Fallin' for An Indianapolis Thug 2

JUDGE & ASARI'S STORY

TINA B.

Fallin' for An Indianapolis Thug 2: Judge & Asari's Story

Published by Grand Penz Publications

Want to be a part of Grand Penz Publications?

To submit your manuscript to Grand Penz Publications, please send the first three chapters and synopsis to grandpenzpublications@gmail.com

Previously...

ASARI GAMES

"You ain't trying to do shit but go be with that new nigga that got you acting funny towards me," I snapped at Kelly as I pulled from the blunt and exhaled. She rolled her eyes on the low and I spinned in the chair so I could finish fixing my makeup.

"What's up, Mercedes? You got that bread?" I asked the new little dancer who had just started working here a few weeks ago.

"Yeah. I was just coming in here to pay you." I smiled and passed the blunt to Kelly. She had a stank attitude because I'd called her out on her shit. She had been acting mad funny toward me lately and I was trying to figure out why. Matter of fact, she'd been acting weird since my aunty and sisters got killed. I get I had a lot going on, but she was moving like she ain't fuck with me.

"Sis, you trippin'. I mean, I have been under my nigga, but you know when you call me I'm coming. You've been moving wild lately. Yo' name is all I've been hearing in the streets," she said, and I rolled my eyes as the dancer, Mercedes, gave me some money in a rubber band. I nodded and slipped it into my purse. I wasn't up for talking to anybody about my personal life. That's exactly what the fuck it was—MY PERSONAL LIFE. Everybody seemed to want to have input on what I had going on, but everybody left when shit got real.

"I'm about to go on stage," I said and tossed one last shot back and stood up. I grabbed all my things, put them into my locker, and gave Kelly the key.

"And actually, I don't wanna go see my nigga. He came up here to see me," Kelly said, and I smirked.

"Matter of fact, he's here now," she said smartly, and I grabbed her arm.

"Let me see him, bitch." I smiled, and she playfully rolled her eyes. As soon as we walked from the back, the DJ called me to the stage.

"There he goes right there," Kelly said, pointing across the room to a VIP section in the back.

"You can't see because he turned around, but come back to his section when you are done," she said and kissed my cheek and ran off towards her nigga. I smiled and headed towards the stairs that led to the stage.

On stage, the curtain was closed, and the music played. I wasn't really in the mood to dance, so I was only doing this show and working the floor for an hour or two.

"I know who y'all came to see. Star Saturdays stay packed to the motherfucking walls. Get motherfucking ready 'cause we got the baddest, rawest bitch hitting the stage RIGHT MOTHERFUCKING NOW! Aye, the homie said y'all can watch and throw money but don't fucking touch. Make some noise for STAR!" the DJ yelled over the mic, getting the crowd hype. I loved working at the club because the club showed me love! Ever since I'd started dancing here, it had been nothing but love and I'd been highly favored.

Once the curtains opened and the beat dropped, all my

worries disappeared. It was like my mind went somewhere else and I went blank.

I felt my body get hot and my breath got caught in my throat, making my eyes pop up. I glanced around the club, thinking Jersey was nearby. My body and mind had their own reactions, and still to this day, it was like my body knew when Jersey was near me. Jersey stood toe to toe with a guy at the back of the club. I thought it might have been the same guy Kelly had pointed to, but I wasn't sure. I couldn't see their faces, but the way they were both standing let me know they were arguing. I saw Jersey nod and smirk, then he made a wavelike gesture and the lights in the club came on, causing the music to stop. Just like that, Dolla yanked me from the stage.

"Homie said get you out of here," he said, wrapping an oversized jacket around my body. Before I could object to Jersey's orders, gunshots rang out, which made Dolla grab me up like a rag doll and carry me out the back door. I saw Jersey's truck waiting for us, so I hopped into the back seat as Dolla got in the front seat.

"Hold on, where is Jersey? Wait for him!" I screamed as the door burst open and people started running everywhere. Dolla hit the steering wheel and grabbed his pistol from under the seat and hopped out and ran back towards the club. My nerves were everywhere. I jumped in the front seat and kicked off my heels. I put the car in drive and grabbed the gun I knew Jersey kept in the glove compartment.

"Fuck, FUCK!" I yelled as more gunshots rang out in the club. The door flew open and the first person I saw was Jersey, easing the scary thoughts that ran through my mind. Right after him were Dolla and June. My heartbeat slowed a little, and I put the car in drive as soon as everybody was in. I sped off as bullets bounced off Jersey's truck. I don't know why, but when I looked back, the eyes I would never forget were staring back at me... with Kelly standing right beside him.

"JUDGE! THAT'S HIM... HE KILLED MY PARENTS."

DIAMOND

"Just ask me anything you wanna know. I promise I'll tell you," Sasha said as I stood straight and stretched my arms. It was five o'clock in the morning and the sun hadn't even risen yet. She had Treasure and I out here training and I didn't understand why. She swore it was to get me mentally prepared for the real world, but Treasure and Jewel had already put me up on game on what they were really into.

My fucking mother was a fucking Queen pin by night and a big-time lawyer who helped other Queen pins by day. When I say my mind was fucking blown, I couldn't believe the shit.

"What made you wanna get into this life?" I asked as I aimed like Jewel had taught me. I aimed at the target and shot three times. Once in the head, and twice in the heart.

"Y'all pops," Sasha said, and did the same as me. She aimed at the head, shot once, then shot twice at the heart. Treasure did the same thing, and we went down the row of 12 Mexican men and executed them right there in the woods.

"Next question?" Sasha asked as we doused the dead bodies with gas.

"What they do?" I asked, and she smirked and looked at Treasure.

"They stole... 100 thousand dollars' worth of cocaine," she spat, and Treasure lit the blunt and passed it to me.

"Am I joining the family business?" I wondered, and Sasha sighed.

"I don't force any of my kids into this. I bring them in, show them what I do, and if they wanna join this life, then that's up to them! Once you get in, you in. Only way you can leave this life is by blood," Sasha said and Treasure nodded.

"So once you die, Jewel takes over?" I asked, and they both laughed.

"Nah. Jewel does his own thing with the guns. I run shit," Sasha said and looked at Treasure.

"You are older than Tres, so you'll take over if you do decide to join us. If not, Tres is next in line. Only way her head won't touch the throne is if she dies!" Sasha let me know and I nodded. I threw the lit blunt into the gasoline and the bodies went up in flames.

"Follow me," Sasha said and we walked a half mile straight into a warehouse.

"If I die today, you'll be up next. You are not ready, so I gotta teach you everything you know about the game," Sasha said as we walked into a big-ass empty room. Only thing I could see was a person's back turned to us, but he was tied up and I couldn't see his face. I only knew it was a guy because his hair was in a low, faded haircut.

"First rule they taught me... always get yo' lick back," Sasha said and handed me a gun. Treasure turned the chair around and it brought me face to face with my brother, Lance. Or I should say, stepbrother Lance...

TO BE CONTINUED...

CHAPTER 1
Judge

"WHAT THE FUCK YOU MEAN HE KILLED YO' PEOPLE?" Dolla yelled from the backseat as I turned around and checked on June. He was in his own little world, but I could tell the shit we'd just found out, had his mind fucked up. Not only was the shiesty bitch Kelly fucking the opps, but the whole time, that nigga June's baby momma was fucking the opps, too! Only way we found out was because the nigga had been hitting too close for us. Whole time, this shiesty ass bitch Tish was fucking this nigga, giving this nigga the drops, the plays, everything! Everything this nigga knew about me, about us, came from his dirty ass baby momma. We wouldn't have even known the shit if he wasn't trying to be funny, talking about how he hit one of our bitches. I knew it wasn't Sari; shorty was only focused on me. Dolla ain't have a bitch and Bird's bitch was 100 percent loyal. Only bitch left was Tish and I was told brother she had been moving funny lately. He was hurt, but I wanted blood. I wanted blood so bad, I could smell it!

Asari was breathing extra hard as she hit a wild ass U-turn in the middle of the street, taking us back toward the club.

"Aye, man, what the fuck you on?" I asked her as she hit the dash back to the club.

"Did you not hear what I just said, nigga? He killed my motherfucking parents!" Asari snapped again as she gripped the pistol I kept in my glove compartment. I had just now noticed she had it in her lap. Shorty was seeing red, and I definitely felt where she was coming from, but I couldn't let her take us back to that hot-ass club, though! There were bodies stretched out everywhere. There was no telling what the fuck we would ride back into.

"I'm going back!" Asari snapped at me, and I ran my hands down my face.

"Yo, pull over, ma," I snapped. "We can't go back there, we just... Man, we can't go back there right now," I told her, shaking my head. My thoughts were running wild, and I just wanted to get the fuck out of this hot-ass truck.

"He... he was with Kelly," she said as she pulled over. I grabbed the pistol out of her hand, put it back in the glove compartment, and got out of the car. Going to the driver's side, I pulled Asari into my arms, and she instantly cried.

"He's back. He really came back." She cried into my chest, and I rubbed her back.

"I got you, ma, just calm down," I told her, not knowing what the fuck was going on.

"Aye, bro, we got to go now," Dolla said. He hopped in the driver's seat while Asari and I got in the car.

"So you telling me this old ass nigga hit our spots, took out a few of our people, killed her parents, fucked my bitch and he's still walking around this bitch freely?" June finally spoke as we rode in silence for a while.

"When did he come back?" Asari finally asked. June looked at me and I sighed. I wasn't about to have this conversation with her. Shit, to be honest, I didn't even know why. I was told a while back he was kin to a nigga I had to get down on, but the facts didn't add up. This nigga just started coming at us for no fucking reason. Either way, this nigga was going to die! I was going to make sure he suffered now that I knew he was the man behind my girl's pain and my shit being fucked with.

"About eight months ago when we first started talking," I told her, and she nodded.

"Why did he come back? Last time I heard, he was gone in the wind," she told me and turned her body towards me.

"What did you do? What did you do to him? Why is he back?" she asked me and we pulled up to the meetup spot.

"Aye, call Bird and tell him to call CP. I need everything on this nigga tonight. June, you're coming with me. D, call me when you make it to the crib," I ordered and dapped Dolla up. I got Asari safely in the car and turned to Dolla. He was on the phone, sending out orders, and I ran my hands down my face. June slid into the car with Asari, and I could see her wipe her tears.

"I'm about to head home, shower, and get my mind right. I'ma slide back past yo' shit in the morning," Dolla said, and we shook up again, then parted ways.

My thoughts were everywhere, but I couldn't even think straight because Asari started asking questions I wasn't ready to answer. My shorty wasn't dumb by far and knew what type of nigga she had, but she also didn't know what type of demon I was behind closed doors. I wanted to keep shit that way. Niggas feared me because they knew I would bust their asses with a quickness. I slowed down because I was focusing on Asari and her family, but trying to make sure shit was good on the home front had me slacking! This new old nigga didn't know who he was dealing with. Niggas were about to see that my demon time wasn't shit to be played with.

* * *

"Love, Loyalty, wake up!" Asari said, running into the house and up the stairs. The whole way to the crib, she was on ten, trying to put pieces together, but I couldn't even help her. I ain't know this old ass nigga or why the fuck he wanted smoke with us. I was the wrong nigga to start a war with, though! My name wasn't Judge for a reason. I was the type of motherfucker who could take your whole fucking life away with one quick bang.

"Sari! Calm the fuck down!" I yelled after her, taking the steps two at a time.

"Love! Loyalty!" Asari said, bursting into Love's room where both girls were sleeping.

"Get up, now!" she roared, and both girls jumped up out of their sleep. Asari grabbed her phone and did something, then shoved it in front of the girls.

"Does he look familiar?" she asked and handed the phone to Loyalty, who was wide awake from all the yelling Asari was doing.

"Sis, how did you..." Love snatched the phone from Loyalty and instantly dropped it and cried.

"That's him! Asari, he killed Aunty!" Love shouted and Asari dropped to the floor with her head in her hands. I picked up the phone and it was the old nigga who had stepped to me reckless in the club.

"He killed our baby sisters," Loyalty said, and looked at me. "How did you get the picture, Sari?" She asked the same question I wanted to know.

"Y'all... he was the one who killed Mommy and Daddy," Asari said as the tears silently fell.

"I think he was trying to kill me," Asari said and looked at me.

BOOM! Gunshots erupted in front of the house, making me immediately cover the girls as best as I could and pull them to the ground.

"What the fuck? Is somebody in here?" Asari yelled, and I put my hand over my lips and pointed to the closet.

"JUNE!" I yelled for my little bro and stood by the door.

"I'm up here, bro!" June responded, and I peeked in the hallway and could see him ducked down by the stairwell.

"Get to the closet," I said, and pulled my pistol out. I saw Love grab something and hand it to Loyalty. Asari pulled a gun from underneath their bed and cocked it back.

"WHAT THE FUCK!" I said and looked at Sari for answers, but she ignored me. Shit, these were some little ass girls, but they were holding pistols like they knew what they were doing.

"Get to the closet and don't come out until I come get y'all!" Asari told them. They crawled to the closet as I jumped up and headed towards the stairs. The gunshots were going off like fucking rockets, but I couldn't tell where they were coming from.

"I think they are coming from the back," Asari said from behind me, and I went down the stairs first. I saw a shadow outside my front window, by the door.

Before I could shoot, two gunshots rang out close by and the figure fell.

"It's him," Asari said as she peeked out the window. I did, too, and saw this old ass nigga, leaned up against his car. He was chilling, smoking a blunt as his peons let their guns bust. Just like a bitch ass nigga to have somebody else pull the trigger.

"Follow me, I got an idea," June said, and I nodded and grabbed Asari's arm. It seemed like the more niggas we dropped, the more niggas came out of nowhere. For the life of me, I couldn't figure out how this nigga knew where I laid my head when only a hand full of people knew. Then, it dawned on me; we had a snake slithering close by! There was no telling what the nigga knew about us.

We headed to the back, and there were two dudes with masks on, trying to come through the door, but June ended that quickly with two shots to the head. I followed him to my garage, and he got into my old school Camaro.

"I'ma get in the car and they're going to be worried about the car and that's when y'all hit 'em up," June said, and I nodded.

"Hell nah, nobody gets in the car. We'll just push the pedal, and we all stay here," Asari said and hit the garage door before we could even say anything, which had me aiming at legs and shooting them dead in the head when they fell. As soon as they noticed the garage door open, they sent a couple of rounds our way.

"Fuck, where he go?" June asked when ol' dude Tez's car was gone, along with his other minions.

"WHAT THE FUCK!" June asked when we looked back at the house and fire and smoke were coming from everywhere.

"WHAT THE FUCK!" I yelled. "Asari! ASARI!" I yelled as she ran back into the house. June and I took after her, and I headed straight up the stairs.

"Asari, Love!" I yelled as smoke filled the air and my lungs.

"We're here. Come on, y'all!" Asari screamed, but I couldn't see shit. I felt Asari touch my arms and heard June yell my name, but my mind was going blank with all the smoke I was inhaling.

"I got him. Help me, y'all," I heard Asari say, grabbing my body as I felt dizzy.

"Asari, he's bleeding. Oh, God, is he hit?" I heard Love say, then hands touched my chest. Once we made it outside, I saw June run towards me and heard Asari scream my name.

"Here comes the fire truck!" Love yelled, and I fell to the ground.

"June, he's been shot!" Asari screamed before everything went black.

CHAPTER 2

Diamond

"Wakey, wakey," I heard and jumped out of my sleep. When my eyes opened, the one face I would never forget was standing over me with the biggest smile on his face.

"What... what are you doing here?" I stuttered and looked around. I was at a loss for words as I jumped up and was surrounded by other inmates in the same place I vowed I would never see again.

"How did I get back here?" I asked, and C.O. James laughed loudly and grabbed my arm.

"You know what you did! You killed that boy. You killed yo' own fucking brother!" he yelled at me, and the tears fell.

"I didn't touch him! I didn't kill anyone!" I yelled, and he grabbed me by the arm and pinned it behind me. In one swift motion, my pants were down around my knees and he had me pinned over my cot.

"No! I'm not letting you do this again. You can't do this again! You can't fucking touch me again!" I screamed as he entered me forcefully, making me scream as loud as I could.

"Fuck," he moaned in my ear as he pushed my head down into the bed harder, my hand still behind my back.

. . .

"Diamond! DIAMOND!" I heard and jumped up from the worst fucking nightmare ever.

"NO!" I yelled.

"Sis, you good. Aye, you good," Jewel said and grabbed me around the arms. He gripped me and hugged me as I let out tears. I didn't know why I was crying; I just knew I was happy to not be asleep. Ever since that day in the warehouse, my dreams had been fucking with me badly.

"Sis, if you need somebody to talk to about that shit, let me know. It ain't easy catching your first body," he said, and chills went down my spine. Little did he know, this wasn't my first body. Motherfuckers didn't know what the fuck we had to do behind those walls. It was survival of the fucking fittest, for real! There was a lot of shit I didn't want to do, but I had to do it! At one point, I thought I wasn't ever coming home. I had to adapt to being behind bars. Now that I was out, on God, they were going to have to kill me before they thought I was going back!

"I don't need to talk to anybody about no bodies! It ain't the bodies that's haunting me..." I said and sat on the bed.

"It's the time you spent behind those walls," he said, reading my mind. I sighed and leaned back. Shit had been moving so fucking fast. One day, I was learning how to protect myself, learning different fighting techniques, and the next day, I was in the middle of nowhere with trained killers, taking out their opps. My life was changing right in front of me. All I wanted to do when I came home was get my payback and start over. Now, I was involved in some other shit.

"Look, I know that look. You having second thoughts about a lot of shit. You don't have to get down with Queenz. Ma don't give a fuck about that shit. It ain't no pressure!" Jewel said and sat next to me.

"I just wanna get my lick back on the motherfuckers who did me wrong. That's all I want," I told him and he laughed.

"Aw, that's mandatory, little sis! You ain't think we were letting those motherfuckers get away with that shit, did you? I know they had something to do with pops! I know it," he said, and I looked at him.

First of all, I couldn't believe I shared my pops with somebody else. The mother who raised me wasn't my real mother. In fact, the bitch who raised me, plotted on me, got me locked up for murder, had my pops killed, and was still walking these dirty-ass streets. I wanted her blood so bad; I could feel it. I guess she wanted me dead, too.

To my knowledge, my pops left me something special, and the only way she could get it was if I was dead. The fact that she made so many attempts on my life when I was locked down was comical to me! I had a powerful Angel watching over me, though. No matter what happened, I was still standing ten toes!

"You got a lot of T's to cross and I's to dot, sis. We got 'em all, though. Everybody gon' die," he told me straight up and I nodded. Still to this day, there was no evidence that Alicia had anything to do with my pops dying. The shit that I found out when I was locked up was more hearsay and what the motherfuckers Alicia had hired said. Once again, there was no evidence, but I knew she'd had my daddy killed. My nigga wasn't going out like no sucker. He had to trust you for you to ever get the ups on him.

"Now, get up and get dressed. We have a meeting to go to and the dukes wants everybody who's anybody to be there!" Jewel said, bringing me out of my head. I nodded and headed to my bathroom that connected to my bedroom.

I was comfortable as fuck staying with Jewel and Treasure. Their house wasn't as big as Sasha's, but their crib was a nice size—four bedrooms, four bathrooms, full basement, and a three-car garage.

They made sure once I was settled in, I had everything plus more. I couldn't lie, the transition from being locked down and then out was hard, but they definitely made it easier for me.

Stepping into the shower, I let the water run over my head and down my body. The training I'd been doing had my body right and tight. I didn't notice how out of shape I was until I was in the middle of fucking nowhere, shooting bears and shit. Getting my aim right, they wanted me to be in the shooting range with the best shooters. They even had me on some sniper shit. Anyway, all the extra fat and meat the prison food put on me turned into muscle. The only good thing that came out of me being locked down was the prison glow. Hair grows longer from no chemicals, teeth pearly white, body stacked. My body on the outside was just right. My mental, though? Fucked up! I had PTSD or something. I was terrified to go back to prison, but then again, I wasn't. I knew the shit I was getting into would have me sitting, but fuck it. I had tunnel vision, and I was ready for whatever at this point.

After washing my hair and washing my body a few times, I stepped out and wrapped my hair and body in towels.

Oiling my body down and handling my other hygiene, I brushed and slipped my hair into a messy bun with a few strands hanging. Slipping on my bra and panty set, I admired my body in the full-length mirror. I had tiger stripes on my ass, and it made me love my body even more. I was stacked as fuck and could bet money people thought I had surgery or something. I slipped on a black, see-through bodysuit with black skinny jeans from Fashion Nova. I applied a bit of makeup and threw on the diamond necklace and matching watch Jewel had gifted me as a welcome home gift. Putting on the final touch, I slipped on black and floral Gucci slides with the matching belt and a matching Gucci tote. One thing I appreciated from Sasha was the upgraded gear. My pops kept me in the latest, and even when I was in college, he made sure I had name-brand shit, but Sasha made sure I had everything and more. Sasha bought me designer shit I couldn't even pronounce yet. I wasn't complaining, though! Any-fucking-thing was better than the grey sweatsuits and black slides I wore while being locked down. She was on a different level than my pops, and I was trying to figure out how the fuck that was even possible. All I'd learned while I'd been out was my pops was something powerful and he wasn't to be fucked with.

Going downstairs, Jewel and Treasure were waiting for me by the door.

"About time," Treasure said, rolling her eyes. I did the same, and when she turned around, I stuck my middle finger up. She opened the door and put her hand out.

"Lead the way." She playfully bowed. I slipped my Gucci shades over my eyes and strutted past her and out the door.

"Bitch," she muttered, and I laughed. Treasure and I were becoming close as hell. At first, it was hard getting used to them because I was bitter as fuck. I'm not going to lie. They didn't give a fuck about my crybaby temper tantrums and ignored when I lashed out. It took for me and Treasure to almost fist fight for Sasha to put me in my place. Well, she didn't put me in my place, but she tried to. I was cool, though, and Treasure was becoming my best friend.

Once Jewel pulled up to the spot, we all got out. I let Jewel go ahead of us and followed him, with Treasure behind me. We rode the elevator in silence and I was nervous as fuck. I'd met a few people who were part of HeadShot Queenz, but I'd never sat in on a meeting before. Jewel wasn't even supposed to be here from my understanding, but I guess Sasha had some important news that called for everybody who was everybody to be in attendance.

Walking into the room, I looked around to peep the scene. Sasha was sitting at the head of the table and there were about ten people sitting around the table, but we separated them into groups of two. Then in the back of the room were about fifteen to twenty niggas.

One couple was a woman and a man; an exquisite couple, might I say. They stood out because they had on white and there was a big-ass white dog laying at the woman's feet. They hit Jewel with a head nod and my attention went to the next person, a woman. I wanted to say her brother because they damn near looked like they could be twins. She was drop-dead gorgeous with the longest blonde hair. The nigga on her side was handsome as fuck, too, but the big ass ring on his ring finger had me minding my business. I wasn't open to any relationship right now, but I could look...

"Welcome my children, everyone," Sasha said, and everyone said their greetings. I sat between Jewel and Treasure and Sasha walked to me and stood behind my chair.

To our left were two females. When I got out, I met one of them. I wanted to say her name was Melody. I didn't know the other chick she was with, but I knew they were sisters. Identical, to be exact. Both were bad bitches, but they gave off a crazy look, and I knew Melody was crazy from the first time we met. Bitch had me in the woods, hunting animals and shit!

"Everyone, this is my oldest, Diamond," Sasha said, and I stood up. The doors opened, and it was definitely the last person I thought I'd see. The dude who sat close to Sasha stood up and hugged her.

"Sorry I'm late, boss lady," Nova said, then looked at me. I smiled and scooted the chair back.

"Diamond?" she asked, walking towards me as we hugged tightly.

"Damn, bitch, you look good as fuck," she said, taking me in from head to toe. I smiled and looked her up and down as well.

Nova was still a beautiful girl. She had picked up a little more weight, but she was still gorgeous as fuck. She had long hair that she wore straight down, past her ass. She was rocking an all-black one-piece that fit her body perfectly, and on her feet were black Louis Vuitton red bottoms. My bitch was moving like a boss!

"You look good as hell, too, man. How have you been?" I finally asked, and my mother cleared her throat.

"I have a few announcements, then you ladies can get reacquainted," Sasha said as she stood behind her chair at the head of the table. I sat in my seat and Nova sat next to her people, I'm guessing, because they both looked Italian.

"Nov, you my girl and all, but next time you come in my shit fashionably late, we gon' have some problems," Ma dukes said, and Nova smiled.

"Yes, Boss Lady," she said, and Sasha nodded.

"Back to what I was saying. This is my daughter, my oldest child. I'm bringing her into this team, this family, and I want everybody to treat her with respect. No, I'm not putting her in a high position. She'll have to earn her spot like everybody else," she said and reached into something under the table. She slid me a phone, and I caught it.

"Everybody has her number, and she has everybody's numbers, too. Since she's already acquainted with Nov, you can let her ride out with you and show her the ins and outs the next few days," Sasha said, and I nodded.

"Now, word around town is shit's about to be hot because motherfuckers are looking for who got Lance's slimy ass out of here. I don't give a fuck what the streets is saying, y'all know what time it is. We got a shipment coming in a few days and this is one of the biggest so far. I need my people on their toes.

They hit, and we hit back harder. I don't give a fuck what we gotta do! They fucked with the wrong motherfuckers, so they gotta go," Sasha said. She walked to a little wall and pressed a button. Lights went off and the black screen lit up with pictures of a group of women. They were beautiful black women, and with the way they dressed and their jewelry, they were definitely African.

"In the meantime, these ladies are our next hit," Sasha said and clicked to the next slideshow.

"Somebody paid two point five million dollars to take out these five bitches! If anybody wants to be put in the pot, let me know. I would like my best hittas on this," Sasha said, and everybody called dibs on that two-point-five.

"I would like Valentina, Rhythm, Queen, Nova, and Tres. Y'all can handle this. Split it four ways. Whatever and whoever you bring in to help is on y'all. I would like this to be handled in the next three days. I'ma send over everything y'all need later on tonight," Sasha said.

"How rude am I? Diamond, this is Queen, and King is her husband. They've been down with me since day one and are the most loyal people on my team," she said and stood between the couple in the white. Queen held her cup up and I smiled.

Next, Sasha stood between the woman with the blonde hair and the dude.

"This is Valentina and Valentine. They handle transportation and get everything we need here with ease. Valentina is gon' be the head of the take down this week."

"Are y'all twins?" I asked, and they both laughed.

"Nah. He is older," Valentina said, and I nodded.

"You know Melody, and that's her sister, Rhythm. Rhy is the head of the Mayweather sisters and there's a few of them, so you're gonna be meeting the other girls later," Sasha introduced and I smiled.

"Yeah, I remember you." I laughed, and Melody laughed with me.

"That's Brazil and his wife. He runs shit with Jewel. That's OG Ciro, Nova's pops. They are just now joining the organization, but I've been knowing OG for a very long time." She smiled and kissed Nova's pops, OG Ciro, on both cheeks. I nodded, and once we all got acquainted and I remembered who was who, she dismissed everybody. Everybody left, and I stood up and Nova pulled me into another hug.

"Damn, man, I've been missing yo' ass!" she told me and I laughed.

"Swear I looked yo' ass up on Facebook, trying to get in touch with you," I told her, and she shook her head.

"I'm not on Facebook, but Instagram, bitch, you can't tell me nothing on there," she said, and we laughed.

"So you rolling out with me?" she asked, and I waved to my people and followed Nova out.

"Aye, Nov!" The one I now knew as Valentina yelled and waved us over.

"Welcome to our team, Diamond," Queen said, and we shook hands.

"Since Boss Lady put you on babysitting duties, we've brought Diamond in on the mission," Treasure said and Nova shrugged, then looked at me.

"You down?" Nova asked, and Treasure smacked her lips.

"Don't let that baby face fool you," Treasure said and Mellody laughed.

"Sis a fool with her tool." Mellody smiled and shook hands with Treasure.

"We can meet up at my compound and go over the shit Bossy sends tonight," Queen said and walked away with nothing else to say. We split up, and I followed Nova outside.

As soon as our feet touched outside, it was like time stood still. My breath got caught in my throat and I felt lightheaded.

The most gorgeous man I'd ever laid eyes on was walking our way. He stood at least 6'5, and his locs were twisted into a style that hung past his shoulders. The golden tips matched his hazel eyes perfectly, and the VVS grill gave him a thuggish look. Tattoos covered the light complexion of his neck and arms and he had big, pink lips and low-cut facial hair that formed into a goatee. Yeah, he was official.

"Wassup, Nov? Who you?" he asked, licking his lips, sending chills down my body.

"Who you?" I mocked, and he smirked and hugged Nova.

"This my bitch Diamond. Diamond, this my cousin Fats, and he also runs with yo' brother," Nova said and he sighed.

"Aw, man, you Jewel's sis? Aw, nope! Unt-unt. Nah, I'm coo', love," he said and started backing up with his hands up in surrender.

"Aye, you my mans' little sis. You fine as fuck, too, but I ain't even on that type of time," Fats said and Nova started laughing. He turned the other way and started to walk off but stopped and came back to where we stood.

"I'm lying, I'll take my chance with him. Can I take you out?" he said and I shook my head at his antics.

"I don't think that'll be a good idea." I laughed and Nova grabbed my arm. I followed her to the car and jumped into the passenger seat.

"This is about to be a long ass day," Nova said. I agreed and pushed my seat back and got comfortable.

CHAPTER 3
Dolla

"Man, what the fuck are you doing here?" I snapped as I walked into my house and my crazy ass egg donor was sitting on my fucking couch again. I couldn't even fucking be mad because I should've moved the first time the bitch, I mean, my momma popped up here. Now she was sitting here with a little smirk on her face, knowing I didn't want her near me.

"Don't fucking talk to me like that! Ya fuckin time is up!" she snapped and I sighed.

"I'm not doing this shit with you! Get the fuck out," I snapped and held the door open for her. She laughed and stood up.

"You don't scare me, boy! I know what you about!" She laughed and I groaned. She acted like she knew what I was about, but if she knew me, then she would've known I was so motherfucking close to breaking her neck.

"Look, what did you really come back for? I'm not about to get in the mix of you and yo' husband's shit! You wanna get at that nigga, do that shit and quit motherfucking trying to come at me about Judge. We solid. I ain't switching!" I told her straight up and she shook her head.

"See, wrong answer... You're gonna wish you had chosen my side. Now I gotta treat you like a nigga on the fucking streets! An opp ass nigga like yo' fucking daddy!" she said and I laughed.

"Bi— Yo, you ain't ever treated me like a fucking son, so please show me how you treat an opp. And as far as my pops, bitch, he stood up as a man and did what he had to fucking do 'cause yo' worthless ass ain't give a damn! Matter of fact, stay the fuck away from me 'cause I don't give a fuck! Come at me again it won't be no talking about shit!" I spat and grabbed her arm. She tried to swing, but I moved back just in time so she missed. I tossed her ass out my front door and slammed it shut.

"I don't know what my..." I didn't know what her issue was with me. I hadn't seen this woman in years. Now, all of a sudden, she was coming around more and more. I knew she was moving grimey as hell from the shit she was spitting, but that shit ain't have shit to do with me! I wasn't changing up on my pops and Judge was solid as they come. If it comes down to it, I'd smoke her ass over my guys. I don't give a fuck about that being my mother. She left me for dead a long time ago, but now she needed my help and wanted to reach out? Fuck her! I ain't have no talk for that egg carrier! She wasn't any mother of mine and her best bet was to stay the fuck away from me.

RING! RING! RING!

I grabbed my phone and immediately groaned, looking at the name. My pops was damn near about to be in the same boat with his baby momma if he ain't get his shit together. Yeah, now that I'm older, motherfuckers get one chance with me, then their waters are cut! I wasn't the same little boy. I didn't care enough to try to mend things with my egg carrier. My pops had more of my respect because he stayed and handled business. He was still just as fucked up as her though in his own ways. My pops cared about the streets and his image more than his kid. Only thing he did was show me how to hustle and get dirty. I wasn't fucking with him like that, though. Especially with my dukes coming back, that was all he was worried about nowadays.

"Yooo," I answered and walked around my crib, making sure nothing was out of place.

"Get to Eskanzi Hospital, ya boy just got hit," my pops said, then the phone went silent. He had hung up. I knew he wasn't talking about Judge because I had just left that nigga not even an hour ago. I dialed Pops back as I grabbed my keys and headed out the door. My pops ain't answer so I dialed Judge, but that went straight to voicemail. After trying him a few times, I dialed Bird's number and he answered on the last ring.

"Yeah," he answered groggily.

"Aye, wake yo' ass up! Nigga, you talked to my boy?" I asked and the line went silent.

"Aw, fuck!" I heard Bird yell and then shuffling around.

"Man, what the fuck!" he yelled again and I drove off towards the hospital. I heard talking on the other end, but I hung up and dialed Judge's number again. I knew my pops' information was true because he was the type of nigga who had the facts with whatever he said. I just hoped my boy wasn't too fucked up or the whole city was going to feel me!

Pulling up to the hospital, I saw the police cars in the parking lot that blocked the main entrance. Going to the emergency area, I parked and hopped out. The first person I saw was June and he was pacing back and forth. Judge's madukes was sitting next to Asari and her sisters. I could tell Asari had been crying and Ma Laura was trying to keep her calm and sane. June met me halfway and we both hugged. I could tell he wanted to say something by the way he looked around but chose not to.

"How is he?" was the first thing that came out of my mouth. June just shook his head and looked down.

"I ain't... I didn't even know the nigga had got hit. He was cool. He had gone back in to get sis nem... I... He was good, bro," June said, and I pulled him into a hug. I heard talking coming from behind us and Bird and the whole gang were walking through the doors.

"What the fuck happened?" Bird, Judge's oldest brother, hissed, and June sighed.

"That old nigga. He came to the crib and lit that bitch up," June said, barely above a whisper, which made Dolla nod.

"Aye, I need you to stay here and look after my dukes," he told me. "Nobody gets close to 'em. Hit my jack when you hear anything," he told me and waved for June and his crew to bounce. A few of them lingered around, just like he told them, but the rest exited with him without another word. I went to Ma Laura and hugged them all before I sat down.

"We ain't claiming nothing. He's good, he's going to be straight!" Asari said and stood up. She started to pace back and forth and only stopped when the doctor followed by another nurse came into the room we were waiting in.

"Family of Jersey Brown," the nurse said and Ma Laura stood up.

"It's us," she said and clasped her hands together.

"How... how is he?" Asari asked and the doctor smiled.

"He's fine. He got hit twice, once in the chest, and another in the back. Neither is life threatening but we had to do surgery to get the bullet out of his chest. He should be up in a few hours and would love to see you guys. Take it easy," the doctor said and walked away, leaving the nurse.

"Only two can go back because of Covid-19," she told us and I nodded at Laura and Asari.

"I'ma sit out here with them." I nodded at Love and Loyalty, who were laying on each other asleep.

"Thank you," Asari said, grabbing Mama Laura's hand as they hurried off. I shook my head and sat down. I grabbed my ringing phone and glanced down at my pops calling.

I shook my head and slipped my phone into my pocket.

"Is Jersey okay?" Love asked and sat up in her seat.

"He's going to be okay. We are waiting for Momma L to come back and she's going to take you to the crib," I told them. Feeling like somebody was watching me, I looked up and around. Shaking my head, my eyes landed on my dukes and she smirked cockily and held up her trigger finger. I stood up but my ringing phone stopped me in my tracks. Looking down at my pops' number again, I groaned and finally answered. Looking around, my dukes was gone.

"Come outside and chop it up with me," he said and hung up. I ran my hand down my face, fed up with all the activities from tonight.

"Stay put, I will be right back." I gave the homie Mack a head nod and walked outside. Most of the police were gone, but I headed towards my pops' truck and slid into the passenger seat.

"I'm trying to figure out why you ain't told me yo' momma was back," was the first question he asked, which made me laugh.

"Nigga, yo' connects tell you everything else. Told you when my boy got hit, but yo' people couldn't let you know yo' baby momma was here? Shit, I thought you knew. Every conversation lately been about her. Yeah, miss me with the dramatics. What's up?" I wanted to know what was up and he wanted to play games.

"How ya mans looking?" he asked and sighed.

"He's good. His ol' lady in there right now," I said and leaned the seat back. He sighed and ran his hands down his face. He wanted to say something but didn't. Taking a good look at my pops, something was definitely up with him. He wasn't dressed up like he usually was when he stepped out. His hair wasn't cut and his facial hair was wild. My pops had always taken pride in his image, so to see him looking down bad had my antennas up.

"Ya mama here for some reason. They say she is trying take over Judge's shit. I ain't in the game anymore, but my information is credible! I try to stay out yo' way and let you do your own thing but the bitch ain't come back 'cause she fucking miss you. You get in this bitch's head and see what she wants from you. Drain that bitch for everything she's worth and got, then send her my way," he said and looked at me.

"I know what she wants. She wants to take over Judge's shit and kill you. The same thing you want," I said and looked at him. My pops was a motherfucker. He always preached and instilled in me how big loyalty was but the nigga didn't stand on the shit. I wasn't getting into the middle of the shit he and his baby momma had going on. They could kill each other for all I gave a fuck! They weren't using me in their games, though.

"I've been trying to help you and young bull!" he said, and I laughed.

"You couldn't possibly believe you keeping tabs on my boy is helping him?" I asked and nodded.

"Just like I told her when she came to see me; I ain't into the weird shit y'all got going on! Y'all wanna kill each other, be my fucking guest! I ain't setting shit up! I ain't picking no side.

Don't let the bullshit y'all trying to plan affect my business and we're all good," I spat and reached for the handle.

"And if I find out either one of y'all got anything to do with my brother getting hit, I'ma pull the trigger myself!" I let him know and slammed the door on my way out of the car.

CHAPTER 4
Chase "Bird" Brown

"Babe, just calm down," my wife said as I did the dash in and out of traffic. I was hitting about ninety on the highway, but my mind was elsewhere. Unfortunately, y'all are only hearing my side due to some misunderstanding! Where I'm from, I'm the one that they call to school these young niggas on how to really handle business! They knew me as the Grim Reaper back in the fucking day! I was supposed to sit this story out and let my little brother have his shine. I ain't wanna be brought into this shit, being the person I used to be. They brought me in when they decided to hit my brother's crib. Now... I had to show everybody that I'm still that same nigga from the bully.

"FUCK!" I snapped and hit the steering wheel. I was 100 hot and only saw red right now. I wanted bloodshed. The streets of Indianapolis knew whatever I wanted, I got. Every-fucking-body knew my little brother was off fucking limits, so I was still trying to figure out why they would have the audacity to touch a hair on his head. They wanted to die!

"Pull the fuck over right now! Nigga, is you fucking

crazy!" my wife Ginger yelled as I came to a prompt stop, making her push up to the dashboard.

"Look, baby, you know I'ma tell you when you moving stupid. We ain't in the street life anymore, nigga, we trying to start a family," she said, then stopped and sighed.

"But you are not in this shit alone. I'm with you. I'm for you and this family. I'm riding with you just like back then! I'm with whatever you want, just let me know if we are all in again," she said. I could tell she wanted to be there for me like how we were back in the day but shit was different now! Shorty had one of my seeds inside of her. I would never let my wife go back to that street life. Busting her guns beside me was what we did when I first entered the game. Yes, over the past years, she had to come out of retirement and stood on some shit, but never would I allow her to this time. Knowing shit was messy and that my little brother was laid up with bullet holes, I couldn't risk that!

"I know what you're thinking, C, but if you think I'm letting you out here without me, you out yo' fucking mind, nigga! I'm the realest motherfucka on yo' team! You forgot I was the only bitch that built that same empire with my bare hands!" she yelled. I laughed and pulled the car over on the shoulder of the highway. The team I had in place pulled up behind me also, three cars deep. I put my hand out the window to let everybody know we were all good.

"I have been laying low, doing my wifey duties and I love it. Nigga, you ain't the only one about to have some fun. Judge is my little brother, too! I wanna see as much bloodshed as you!" she said, and as soon as she opened the door to get out, gunshots rang out, making me grab her by her hair into the car. I pulled my pistol out and hit the gas, chasing after the motherfucker who'd just rode past, spraying the car with bullets.

Thank God the first investment I'd made when I purchased this whip was making it bulletproof.

"What the fuck!" Ginger yelled when two cars pulled alongside us and rolled the window down with pistols busting our way, hitting my side of the car. My wife hopped in the back and pulled the Micro Draco AK from under my seat. She wasted no time letting the back window down, barking that bitch!

I saw my crew behind us, getting to it. Shit was wild as fuck. All the fucking years I'd been in this life, I'd never been in a wild ass shootout on the fucking highway. A hot-ass highway, to be exact. If we made it out this bitch, which I knew we would, we were liable to get ran the fuck up by the jakes.

"Babe, fall back. Aye, fall the fuck back!" Ginger yelled, which made me slow the car down and hit the nearest exit. Once I saw my men in the back of us, I detoured and pulled to the closest duck-off spot I knew about. Jumping out the car, Ginger stayed back as my boys hopped out, talking shit.

"Aye! Aye, man!" I yelled, trying to get their attention.

"I don't know what the fuck that shit about, man! I don't fucking know what the fuck is going on, I just know my wife was this close... this fucking close to getting her brains splattered on the inside of my fucking car! Listen the fuck up. Every nigga right here, right now, hit the streets! I wanna know who and where! Do not call my phone if y'all don't got a name and location! Shit is about to get real fucking ugly. Pull bro's shit from the streets. Pull his men from the spots! All water is cut the fuck off. A lot of blood gon' shed until I get my answers! I need everybody in these streets right now, and if any nigga don't wanna get down, lay 'em down! Simple as that," I snapped, ready to break anybody's neck. I was on ten and the only thing that calmed me down was Ginger grabbing my shoulder. Even though I towered over her like Big Foot, her simple touch made me simmer down and briefly forget about what had just happened.

"You should get back to the hospital. Take me home," she said softly, which let me know she was real deal pissed the fuck off.

If anybody knew Ginger and me, she was my heart in human form. Only person in this world I loved more than myself. She came first with everything and anybody!

Gin and I had been together since we were twelve and fourteen. She was my best friend first, though, since we were jits. Now that we were hitting our thirties, I wanted something more, something different.

Ginger was the most beautiful girl I'd ever laid eyes on. Standing at 5'6, all legs, she was thick as hell, too, with deep dimples on each side that showed with every facial expression. She had a short cut that she'd been rocking since a kid, and I loved that shit.

My girl was smart as fuck. Even with us rocking the streets, shorty went to college and graduated with her master's. Even cleaned all my money up through several daycares she had throughout the city.

I definitely had a rare gem and didn't hesitate to lock her down as soon as we turned eighteen.

"I'ma head to the crib. Y'all get on with what I said to do." I dismissed these niggas and headed to drop Ginger off at the crib.

* * *

Back at the hospital, I stood by Judge's bed as Asari slept in the chair on the other side.

My boy was sleeping, but every now and then, I saw his body jerk and that made me touch his hand.

"Nigga, don't try to hold my hand," he said, barely above a whisper, which made me laugh.

"Fuck you, nigga. Get yo' ass up, so we can hit these fucking streets!" I snapped and Judge sighed heavily.

"It ain't as easy as it seems... Bro, I can't fucking walk," Judge hissed. I saw the anger in his eyes and looked at Asari.

"She doesn't know?" I asked and he shook his head.

"Nah. I told the doctors not to say anything. I'm fucked up," he told me, and I grabbed a chair and pulled it next to the bed.

"Are they saying it's permanent?" I asked, wondering what the fuck went wrong.

"I don't know. As soon as they said some shit about walking, I spazzed," he said and I nodded.

"Nigga, can you feel yo' legs?" I asked and he shook his head no.

"Tell Sis... she's gonna ride regardless, little bro! I know," I said, but the look he gave me made me think otherwise. Only I knew how he felt about Asari. Let's just say that was one thing we had honest—loving hard. I understood why he wanted to wait, but the longer he waited, the worse it'll be to explain.

"I... Have they found out anything about ol' dude?" Judge said, trying to sit up. I stood to help but he held his hand up, stopping me.

"I'm good, bro. How's June?" Judge asked and I shook my head. With the shit that happened on the highway, and making sure my family was straight, I hadn't even checked on lil bro.

"Let me get out of here and check on that nigga. He probably killed Tish and set the whole motherfucking house on fire with her in it," I said, shaking up with him. I could tell there was something else on his mind, but he opted not to say anything, which had me leaving him with his own thoughts.

CHAPTER 5
Asari

"Grand rising, king." I smirked and opened the curtains for Jersey. The way he mugged me let me know he was in a mood today. I rolled my eyes and went to sit next to him on the bed.

"What's wrong?" I asked and he just looked at me, then turned his attention to the TV that wasn't even turned up. This had been his attitude since he'd woken up from surgery. Yeah, shit had been fucked up with us, but seeing him drop like that in my arms, I thought he was gone. I just knew he was gone! Death had been a friend of mine for a very long time, and it only seemed like God took the ones I loved the most away. I was so scared to love again, so scared to open my heart up and let him in. I was afraid he was going to be snatched away from me and there wouldn't be shit I could do about it. So, yeah, shit was fucked up between us because of me, but shit, we almost lost our fucking life. He shouldn't be bitter with me; we should be cherishing each other right now.

"What's wrong with you?" I asked again and he sighed.

"Nothing, Asari. Trying to watch this show but you keep talking," he spat and I laughed. I sat up on the bed and turned to look at him. Even with the bandages on his chest, face, and legs, Jersey was still the fucking sexiest man I'd ever laid eyes on. His dreads were pulled up into a ball at the top of his head, showing his face. Even with the new scars that lined his face from the war the other night, he was still a piece of art. I could tell he was in deep thought about something because his jawline tensed up and he started to bite the inside of his jaw.

"Just talk to me! What's going on?" I pleaded after a moment of silence. He sighed and leaned his head back into the pillow.

I stood up and started to pace the floor, ready to explode. I had been up here at this hospital since day one, day and night, only leaving for a few hours every other day to go check on the twins. Still, he treated me like it was my fault he was in the hospital. I felt like he was being so motherfucking inconsiderate.

"Look, the doctors said I might not be able to ever walk again," he spat. I knew that was where the hurt was coming from. His eyes held so much pain. I put my head down to stop the waterworks. He looked at me, but when the tears filled my eyes, he looked away and shook his head.

"I don't need ya tears. I don't need ya sympathy!" he said and I shook my head. I went to the door to get a nurse.

As I made it to the nurse's station, the doctor was walking up also.

"Hello, Ms. Games, how is my patient?" he asked, and I sighed, wiping the tears.

"Is it true that he won't be able to walk again?" I asked and he sighed.

"No, that isn't true. Mr. Brown is a stubborn man. He doesn't even get out of bed. I scheduled for him to start physical therapy two days ago and he hasn't made any effort to go. When his nurse comes to get him, he doesn't even acknowledge her. If Mr. Brown wants to walk again, he has to get up," he said, and I nodded.

"Can I take that?" I asked and he nodded. Once I got what I needed, I went back to Jersey's room and he was staring into space. He hadn't even noticed I was back in the room.

"So, what you thought, I was just going to dip out once you told me that?" I asked and his facial expression softened a little.

"This is yo' fucking problem. This room, this hospital. Get out of bed, come on," I said as I locked the wheels of the wheelchair and went to move the cover off of Jersey. He was still dressed in the hospital gown. I went to the closet and grabbed the bag of clothes I had brought for him last week. Grabbing some sweats and a matching jacket, I sat him all the way up. Taking one leg at a time, I swung them to the side of the bed as he watched me carefully. After successfully dressing him, he threw his arm around my neck. Three successful attempts to get him to stand, he stood to his feet with me holding him up.

"Grab ahold of the bed, and we gon' turn together," I said, but he didn't respond. Once we got him into the wheelchair comfortably, I handed him his phone and a pillow. Under the pillow was his gun, so I handed it to him, and we went out the door.

"I don't know what God has in store for you, but you can't let this shit get to you. You gon' be walking again! As long as you go to yo' physical therapy. And I'm trying to figure out why the fuck you ain't been going. Ain't told nobody shit or nothing!" I asked and stopped in my tracks when he didn't respond. Turning him to me, I squatted down so we could be at eye level.

"Look, it's some shit I don't like speaking on. I haven't been the same since my sisters and aunty died! Who would? That's not an excuse, but I'm sorry for the way I've been acting. I've experienced so many deaths, Jersey. I was scared as fuck, I thought I had lost you. Right now, that's something I can't take," I expressed and he nodded. I grabbed his hand and stood up to hug him. My eyes locked with the eyes I never wanted to see again in life.

"Jer-Jersey," I stuttered and released him from my arms. He turned his chair around, trying to see what I was looking at, and I saw Tez clear as day whisper something to his homie to the left and the whole crew turned our way.

"What... what do I need to do?" I whispered. Judge moved his hand under the pillow slowly. I grabbed his shoulder so he could stop before he got us both killed.

"I'm about to kill this motherfucka!" he spat and I stood in front of him. I leaned down and kissed his lips.

"You gotta calm down, baby. You can't do shit in a hospital full of people. He can't do shit, either. Fuck him for now. When you get back A1, then you handle him," I said and he nodded, biting the inside of his jaws. I stood in front of him and he looked into my eyes. I saw him slowly calming down, and when I moved out of the way, Tez and his crew were gone.

"We getting the fuck up out of here! Today," I told Jersey as he typed on his phone. I pushed him back to his room.

"See, these motherfuckas is being real fucking bold, man!" June yelled and I sighed. We were back at Jersey's momma's house and I was fed up with the hollering. Everybody talked about what they were going to do or what needed to be done. Still, the motherfuckers who set Jersey's house on fire, shot him, and killed my whole fucking family was still out there, roaming the city without a care in the world.

"They been bold, nigga! They were motherfucking bold when he went to little bro's spot!" Chase yelled and I sighed and stood up.

"I ain't trying to be in y'all business," I started to say.

"Well, don't," Jersey spat, and I laughed. He mugged me and I mugged him back. I didn't know why this nigga was so mad at me. He wheeled himself to the other side of the room and mugged me from afar. I didn't give a fuck. This was Jersey's attitude all day.

"You niggas been yelling since Jersey got out of the hospital!" I said as I saw Jersey's momma standing in the doorway.

"If y'all wanna get at this nigga, y'all need to get at him through whatever bitch got his heart! I'm not going to be sitting for long. I want bloodshed and I want it, now. He took too many of my loved ones. Brought me out of the comfort of my own house! I'm not laying down anymore. Shit gotta change!" I spat and looked at Jersey. He wanted to be mad at me but whatever he did to that nigga had brought that nigga back! Yeah, I didn't know why this nigga had come for my family, but apparently, he was on two different times! He wanted beef with me for his own fucking reason, then he wanted smoke with Jersey and his people for another fucking reason.

But just like he did me, I'ma do him! I'ma take every fucking family member he has left! Walking over to Jersey, I kissed him on the cheek and he grabbed my arm.

I wasn't up to sit and talk about this shit right now. I knew where I wanted to start and the shit that everybody was doing right now wasn't going to set shit in motion. That nigga Tez was up one tremendously. I didn't know who the fuck had given him the fucking courage to think he was running shit but I wasn't letting that shit ride with my sisters! He had to pay, and I was taking out the first person we had in connection!

CHAPTER 6
Judge

"I feel like a hoe, man." I groaned as I did another crunch and stood. My thoughts were getting the best of me, and I had to hit the gym. I was back in the field, but I laid low. I wanted my health to be back to 100 percent. It had been about six weeks since I'd been shot. Just like the hoe ass nigga he was, he was back in the wind.

"You should," Dolla spat and we both looked at each other. Dolla hopped up and we stood in each other's faces.

"The nigga hit the club… twice! Nigga, you would've deaded that shit the first time he tried to get at us. You slacked! You went out of town, nigga! You should've handled that nigga first. While you were out of town, he hit Bird's club, hit yo' girl's spot, and hit our spot! It took you getting shot and him burning yo' shit down to the ground for you to make a move. Bro, you let him slide too many times," Dolla said and I nodded.

"We even closed shop… As much money as I've been making with you, we ain't ever did that shit! This nigga got you changing everything!" Dolla roared and kicked the stand, making some shit fall.

"Yo' shorty was right. We gotta hit this nigga some way, somehow," he said and I stood there, taking everything in.

"Well, you make the next move then and make the next move the best move. I'ma call one of my guys and get some shit in motion," I told him, then paused.

"As far as the spot? Ain't shit moving in this motherfucking city until that nigga's dead. You mad you ain't eating, nigga? Get in the fucking streets and apply pressure to niggas," I said and he nodded. We shook up and I pulled him into a brotherly hug.

"You heard from yo' dukes?" I asked and he shook his head no.

"She is lingering 'round. Fill me in on the plan yo' pops cooked up," I said and sat down. I started to do my leg exercise as he explained all the shit he found out about his people, and how he was going to get at both of them.

After Dolla and I chopped it up for a few, I headed to my dukes' crib. Since my shit was burnt down, the safest place was my momma's shit. I had a meeting with some realtor later who Chase did business with. I was hoping Asari would come with me, but shit between us was off. I knew when shit turned bad with us, but I ain't think shit was this bad! Shorty couldn't even stay in the same room with me unless we were arguing.

It was so bad; I was staying out in the streets all day and only came home to shower and sleep. She would already be asleep when I got to the crib and I'd be out of the house by the time she got up.

Pulling up to my dukes' crib, I parked next to a U-Haul. I saw Asari standing with Love and Loyalty and they looked like they were arguing.

"You can take that shit somewhere else! Y'all not moving unless I say so! Now help get this shit," Asari spat and Love walked away, but Loyalty stood in front of her. I grabbed Loyalty and she was about to say something.

"What's up? What's going on?" I asked as two men walked around me with bags in their hands.

"I can't do this shit! I can't!" Asari yelled and Loyalty smacked her lips.

"You can't do what? I didn't ask you to do shit! I don't want this fucking life! I hate fucking living!" Loyalty yelled and Asari reached back and smacked her clear across the face.

"You ungrateful as fuck, yo. I been breaking my fucking neck for y'all, for us, since I was fourteen years old! Bitch, I'm fucking tired!" Asari yelled and Loyalty looked at her with tears in her eyes.

"I didn't ask you to! You could've left us! Bitch, Aunty, and OUR little sisters would still be here! It's yo' fucking fault we orphans! It's yo' fucking fault my baby sisters not here! FUCK YOU! The least you could do is fix what the fuck you did!" Loyalty yelled and Asari tried to charge at her, but I grabbed Asari as she tried to get to Loyalty. We both stopped when we heard a gun cock.

"I let you slide once. Don't put yo' hands on me again," Loyalty spat, holding the gun towards Asari.

"Put the fucking gun down, Loyalty!" Love yelled from the doorway. Loyalty looked at Love and dropped the gun.

"I'm... I'm sorry," she tried to say, but Asari was on her ass in one swift motion. Asari had Loyalty on the ground, her legs pinning her arms down.

"Bitch, don't you ever in yo' fucking life pull a fucking gun out on me! Are you fucking crazy?" Asari yelled as she threw punch after punch. Love came out of nowhere and grabbed Asari by the hair, but that didn't stop her. She wrapped her legs around Loyalty, dragging her as I grabbed Loyalty.

"CHILL THE FUCK OUT!" I yelled and pushed Loyalty

back as she ran up on Asari and hit her two times, drawing blood from Asari's nose. That turned Asari up more, and when she turned to hit Love, I grabbed her arm midair and shoved her to the ground.

"CHILL THE FUCK OUT!" I roared.

"FUCK YOU, JERSEY! Get the fuck off me!" Asari yelled and stood up.

"I'm done! I'm so fucking done with all this bullshit!" Asari yelled and went into the house.

"Y'all good?" I asked Love and Loyalty. Love was silently crying, and Loyalty just looked in space.

"I'm out! Since I'm the blame for everything and y'all hate me so fucking much, I'm out!" Asari said, wiping the tears that fell from her eyes.

"Come on, man. Asari!" I tried to grab her and she yanked away from me and mugged me.

"Fuck you, nigga!" she yelled and jumped in her shit and pulled off.

"Y'all might as well put all that shit back. Shorty pranked out!" I told the movers and they just stood there, looking around.

"Y'all fucking slow? Put that shit back! Shorty not going no-fucking-where!" I spat and they scrambled back to the truck.

"Where you get this shit from?" I asked Loyalty and handed her her little pistol back.

"My friend," she spat and I shook my head.

"Man, come on in here," I said and they followed me to the kitchen where my dukes was moving around like there wasn't a scuffle going on outside her front door.

"Ma, now you know you could have helped me defuse that," I said and she looked at me and kept doing what she was doing.

"Girls, go up there and get cleaned up. I'm making some

food for y'all," she said and they both walked away as I sat at the table.

"Asari getting on that girl's ass was well fucking needed! She's been letting them do too much around here. You know like I know that was inevitable. Now all that other shit, I'm not getting in! She's the big sister. I love Asari and she only does what she knows how to do. What that little girl said to her was so fucking wrong, Jersey," she spat and I sighed.

"Don't you have somewhere to be?" she asked me and I grabbed my phone. It was dead, so I headed up the stairs, put my shit on the charger, and hopped in the shower.

Dressed down in a gray Palms Angel sweatsuit, I slipped my feet into all-white Ones. I grabbed my phone and headed downstairs, but not before grabbing Love and Loyalty so they could ride with me.

"Do you think she's gonna come back?" Loyalty asked me.

"I don't know. Have you tried calling her?" I asked and she sighed.

"Yes, called and texted a million times. I was just so pissed. She has never hit me before," Loyalty said and Love sighed. I could see who was the leader out of the two and looked at Love in the rearview mirror.

"You didn't have to say that. Asari... Asari is different now. You know that, Loyal!" Love said and sat back in the seat.

"You went overboard saying that shit, but if you feel like that, you need to talk to your sister about the shit. Y'all getting older now. Y'all know what type of life she's trying to keep y'all away from. What the fuck was you thinking pulling a gun out, shorty? Come on, now. If you pull a gun out on anybody, you gotta fucking use that shit! If you were in the streets, the same streets she begs you to stay out of, shorty, you would've been smoked!" I told her straight up and she looked at me.

"I'm sorry—" she started to say but I cut her off.

"Don't apologize to me. You hurt her, not me. You fucked

up her head with the shit you spit, not mine! I don't condone no fuck shit Asari be on, but we all you got, shorty! She's all y'all got! So when she ain't fucking with you, I ain't fucking with you! You ain't ask her to look after you or make sure y'all stayed together, but she did a good job doing it," I said. I wasn't going to sugarcoat shit with them. That's the problem, Asari wanted them to stay babies when they were grown as fuck out here in the streets, just like Asari was. Yeah, they were sneaky with their shit, but I knew everything! I just didn't bring the shit to Asari because shorty had hella shit on her plate. That's why every chance I got; I had a sit down with them. Loyalty was so headstrong. She made up her mind a long time ago that the streets was what she wanted. Love, she wasn't like that! I could see it in her face, in her eyes that she didn't want this!

"So, what's ya move then? Y'all got everything figured out, so what's next?" I wondered.

"What you mean?" Love asked, sitting up, leaning on the middle console. I saw she was now intrigued by the conversation.

"Whatever you think I mean," I told her.

"To be honest, we gon' handle it! We gon' get the bitch Kelly first. She gon' lead us right to the nigga!" Love spat and I nodded.

"Then what? Y'all gon' smoke him?" I wanted to know and Loyalty scoffed.

"What, you think we can't?" she asked and I laughed.

"Not with that little ass .22 you got. Second, y'all ain't ever caught a body. How y'all know y'all about that life?" I asked as we pulled up to the address I was given.

"Shit, the scariest nigga can kill. It ain't catching the body we scared of," Love said and looked at Loyalty.

"It's getting out alive for me," she said, looking at me.

"We can get close to the nigga... We have before," Love said and I snapped my neck, looking at her.

"What the fuck you mean, you have before?" I snapped and Love looked at Loyalty, then back at me.

"I've been talking to his nephew. He goes to my school. He took me to his spot one day. I've met the nigga. He knew who I was but he doesn't know that I know him," Love said and I nodded.

"So y'all wasn't gonna say shit? What if he would've killed you?" I yelled and Love jumped.

"But he didn't! I'm still fucking here!" she snapped.

"I know where the fucking spot at. I just need somebody to get me out of there safely. I wanna be the one to take his life... just like he took mine," Love spat and Loyalty turned to me.

"We need you. We can give you everything we know on this nigga!" Loyalty said and I shook my head.

"Oh, y'all gon' tell me every-fucking-thing but I ain't putting ya in the field. Are y'all fucking crazy! This ain't no fucking game. Niggas are fucking dying every day.. and y'all just sitting on information that could have led me to him this whole time!" I shook my head and picked up my phone.

"If we can't go with you, I ain't telling nothing. I'ma get it one way or another!" Love said and I was stunned to even hear baby girl talk so much. I shook my head.

"Where we at?" Love asked and I pulled my ringing phone out.

"Yo..." I answered for June. My mind was blown at the conversation I'd just had with these little ass girls. I couldn't even see the nigga Tez being so fucking careless that he'd be around them. That shit didn't sit well with me.

"What's the word?" he asked.

"Can't call it. I'm out handling this little move right quick. You get that information for me?" I asked and he groaned.

"I'm getting to it. I'ma hit you back in an hour, though. I just got the lo on this hoe and need you to slide down with me," June said and we disconnected the call. June was in the streets heavily trying to find his baby momma. I didn't know what he was going to do when he found her, either, but I knew she had crossed the line and had to stay there.

Parking in the circular driveway, a white 2020 G-Wagon pulled behind mine and two women hopped out.

"Yeah, whose house is this?" Love asked, looking in the back. I laughed and opened my door.

"Come on, get out," I told them and they both hopped out quickly.

"Hi, you must be Jersey. I'm Brailee, and this is my assistant, Nicole. Thank you for allowing me to show you a few of my properties. You said you were looking for a spot that's ducked off. Here you have two acres of land both ways and we are in the process of building a twelve-foot steel gate for security measures. This home also includes a three-car garage, outdoor pool with a three-bedroom, two-bathroom pool house, six bedrooms, eight bathrooms, a full basement, plus a game room. This house was built about fifty years ago and was just remodeled five years ago. It is a little pricey but it's worth it."

"Are you trying to buy this for you?" Love asked and I looked at them as they looked around in awe.

"For us! All our names would be on the deed. This is gonna be our house," I told them and they smiled.

"We should take a tour," Brailee said and ushered us to the front door.

"We have regular locks, but an extra security precaution is this lock pad. You'll set a four-digit code and it'll unlock this front door and the middle garage. I love this door; it's huge and heavy," she said and pushed the door. Not going to lie, walking into the house was something I only saw in movies.

The ceiling was very high, there were spiral stairs, and large, floor-to-ceiling windows. Yeah, this was the one.

"I like this," Love said and walked off with Loyalty, looking around. After going from room to room, we'd finally made it to the master bedroom. Opening the double doors, I grinned. The room was open, and very spacious. I saw a balcony next to the closet, and on the other side of the room, was a full his and hers bathroom.

"I can tell by your facial expression you like it," Nicole said and I smiled.

"Hell yeah, I like it. My girl is going to love this, too," I said and thought about Asari. She wasn't fucking with me right now, but we were locked in. There was no way she was leaving me.

"Damn, ya girl? I was hoping you were single," Nicole said and Love scoffed.

"Yeah, he's dating my sister, so move around... Yeah, I don't like this house," Loyalty snapped and I laughed.

"What's the closing price?" I asked, ignoring Loyalty's little tantrum.

"Well, they are asking for 750,000," Brailee said, walking in with Love as Love asked her a lot of questions about the house.

"Are you sure you don't wanna look at other places? They're in the same price range and I just save they're one story but very spacious," Brailee said as she typed on her phone.

"Nah, we gon' take this one," I said and she clapped.

"Okay, so with you getting this property today, let me run down a few things we would need," Brailee said and I nodded for Love and Loyalty to follow us as she started to run down the prices and everything I needed.

After closing the property and wiring the money to her bank, I was handed the keys to our new spot. We headed out.

"Y'all wanna stop and grab some food? I gotta head somewhere, so I'll drop y'all back off," I said and Love shrugged her shoulders.

"Yeah, that's coo'. Can we get takeout at Outback?" Loyalty said and I nodded.

Ring! Ring! Ring!

I sighed and grabbed my jack and it was my homie, Biggie. He owned the club Asari used to work. She hadn't been back since the little shit that happened and wasn't going back. Biggie was kind of heated. I had pulled his best dancer off the pole, but shit, it is what it is. I didn't need to do business with that nigga anymore anyway; he had too many opp niggas around his spot.

"Talk to me," I answered on the last ring.

"Judge, my man, ya woman just came in. But I need you to get here fast or send some people 'cause ya boy just walked in right after her," he let me know and I hit a U-turn in the middle of the street.

"Aye, get her to your office, and don't let nobody near her," I snapped and hopped on the highway. After hanging up, I dialed June and Dolla to meet me at the club. They were around the way, so they headed there. I just prayed they got there fast because I was a good thirty minutes away. If that nigga touched a hair on shorty's head, his whole family and anybody who was with him family was going to feel me.

CHAPTER 7
Asari

Standing at the bar, I took another shot and looked around the club. Since it was early, it was kind of dead but it was a cool little crowd.

"Glad to have you back, Star," the bartender, Lacy, said, and I smiled.

"Girl, I ain't back, I just came to have some drinks. I got too much shit going on." I sighed and ordered another shot. I was in my feelings bad. The hot shit that Loyalty had said had fucked me up.

Growing up, all I wanted was to take back the night my dad made me take him to Tez. I wish I could do that whole day over again. I couldn't and I'd dealt with it my whole life. I thought I was doing what I was supposed to do. I made sure my siblings and I stayed together. I'd been taking care of them little girls since I was a fucking kid myself. Yeah, my aunty got us together, and I wasn't taking shit away from her, but I'd held it all together. It was me! I made doctor's appointments and hair appointments. I stood in the rain, snow, sleet, and hail for those little girls! For US! So, yeah, I was in my feelings bad because my life had changed in so little time. Everything wasn't great but we were finally okay. We were living and moving on from losing our parents, but now shit was even harder. I had my sisters to keep me grounded and on a straight path, though, but I felt like I'd failed them, and now Love and Loyalty weren't fucking with me. I was sick and tired of being sick and tired.

"Star! Bitch, you hear me calling you?" Lacy yelled and I nodded.

"Girl, I zoned out. I'm feeling these little shots." I laughed, trying to shake my feelings. My head was pounding and my heart was slowly breaking. I had never felt like my life was out of control until now.

"Bitch, what the fuck happened? Yo' nigga took you from the pole to the mansion?" She laughed, but I didn't find it funny.

"Lacy, I'm only nineteen years old. Bitch, the pole wasn't my resting place," I snapped and she laughed.

"No offense, I'm just saying. That nigga came in here once or twice before you started working here. He snatched your little chocolate ass fast!" she said and I smiled, thinking about the night Jersey and I met. It was really love at first sight. The way he burned a hole into me was what made me give him a chance. I knew the nigga was dangerous. Even with him being in the streets, something in my soul told me everything was my fault. My aunty's and sisters' blood was on me. I felt it. What I saw that day, I was supposed to die behind. I just didn't understand why he came back for me after all this time. I was so stuck and confused. For the life of me, I couldn't understand what that nigga Tez wanted with me!

Thinking back to when I first met Tez, I was only thirteen and he was eighteen. Don't ask me what the fuck I was doing trying fuck with a grown ass thug like him. Fucking with Kelly's ass. Ironic. She was messing around with his homeboy and had brought me around their crew. From that day, Tez and I were just cooling it. He always stressed how we couldn't have sex because I was too young and he wasn't that type. He was just drawn to my mind, demeanor, and the way I carried myself differently than the bitches from the hood. I thought I was special. Looking back now, that nigga was gaming the fuck out of my young ass. How different could my young ass be compared to bitches his age and caliber? I was stuck and in love, until that fucking night.

I snuck out of Kelly's window and went to find Tez because he had been ignoring my phone calls. I went to the spot where I knew he hung out. I had never gone there before but the streets talked. That was the hot spot for Tez and his crew. He always said he didn't want me to come around and something happen that I couldn't get out of. Going over there, I didn't care about what might happen. My nigga was well known and wouldn't let anybody touch a hair on my head. Besides, my pops had earned his stripes in the hood. Everybody knew me as Ace's daughter or the little momma who ran with Tez, so I was good anywhere I went.

As soon as I walked into the house through the back door, I saw firsthand why he didn't want me around. This nigga had his dick in another nigga's ass. I was so disgusted, yet I stood in the doorway, looking. Vomit flew out of my mouth so fast, I didn't even notice that Tez had spotted me and jumped up, covering himself. He tried to grab me but I was too quick and ran out the back door. The whole way to Kelly's, I cried. I was so disgusted. Before I could make it back to Kelly's house, my momma rolled up on me, dragging me back home. Everything went downhill from there and my parents were killed the same night.

"Word around town, some niggas from the Ave want ya mans dead. He frequents the club often. You know I try to keep myself out of the mess," Lacy said, letting me know she didn't want her name to be brought up. She knew how Judge got down so I was pretty sure she was just scared and I nodded.

"You got a location, where he hangs out or anything?" I asked, feeling goosebumps form. I didn't know why, but the hairs on my neck started to stand, which made me look around. Nothing seemed out of the ordinary, but now I wished I hadn't come to the fucking club. Especially with this crazy ass nigga running round. Trust, if Lacy was speaking on some shit, that meant it was the hottest topic around this motherfucker.

"Matter of fact, bitch, the nigga used a fucking card. Hold on," Lacy said and went to the back. She slid me some paper and I snapped a picture and sent it to Jersey.

"Hey, Kelly," Lacy said and I froze as I felt a figure next to me.

"What's up, Lacy? Let me get a shot of Remy," Kelly said and I finally looked up. When she finally looked at me, her face drained and she backed up a little. I didn't know what had happened, but I immediately jumped on her and started hitting her. I felt a hit from the side but that didn't stop me; it turnt me up more. I felt Kelly hitting me but it didn't faze me. I felt a yank to my hair and turned around, raining blows on the bitch who had walked up with Kelly. The bitch looked so familiar, but I didn't give a fuck. Whoever was hanging with this bitch was an opp to me! She was catching these hands just for being cool with a fake ass slime like Kelly.

"Aye," I heard and was thrown to the ground. The wind was knocked out of me, and I was yanked up by my hair. I turned to swing but stared right into the eyes of the devil himself. He laughed and looked down, and that was when I felt the warm liquid running down my legs.

"You know you fucked up, right?" he asked and started dragging me out of the club as I screamed and kicked. Nobody helped, though. Everybody just stood around and watched this big-ass nigga drag me out the door by my hair. I looked at Lacy and she was already on her phone, walking after us slowly.

Tez threw me in the backseat of a car and slid in next to me. I hopped up on him and started hitting him. It was like my little fist didn't work because he was so unbothered. In one swift motion, he backhanded me, sending me falling into the door, making blood gush from my nose. I grabbed the door handle but it didn't open so I started to pound on the window. I saw Lacy taking pictures and started to cry.

"HELP!" I screamed and saw Dolla hop out of a car and start to run to the club.

"DOLLA! HELP!" I screamed, banging on the door. He stopped and looked directly at me. June came out of nowhere, firing at the car as the driver sped off with me banging on the window.

"We meet again, Little Miss Asari," Tez said and hit me in the head with the butt of his gun, knocking me out cold.

* * *

"Ahh!" I screamed as a big ass rat ran across my feet. I tried to kick but my feet were tied to the bedpost. Both wrists were tied to a bedpost, and I could barely move. My body was stretched in the shape of an X and I saw the bruises all over my skin. Wherever I was was cold and stinky. I didn't have any clothes on but my bra and panties. I could tell my body had been untouched because I didn't feel any pain or discomfort in between my legs.

"Help, pleaseee!" I yelled and heard a bang. I knew I wasn't alone in this dirty ass motherfucker just from the muffled sounds and stomping above my head.

"HELP ME, PLEASE!" I screamed.

"Bitch, shut the fuck up!" I heard from the other side of

the door. I started to cry louder, then I heard steps. The door swung open, and I saw Kelly come in with another chick. The same chick I had pounced on at the club.

"Bitch, you doing all that fucking screaming," the chick said and I saw Kelly wrap something over her hands.

"Bitch, shut the fuck up."

Whap. Whap.

Kelly had hit me with a two-piece dead in the face, dazing me a little. I could taste blood in my mouth and ran my tongue over my front teeth and started to smile. I was so fucking pissed they had caught me slipping like this. All I could do was take whatever they gave me. Judge had warned me hella times not to go out by myself, and to watch my back. The tears welled up in my eyes, but I refused to let them fall. I knew how the game went. The streets ain't love nobody!

I didn't expect anybody to help me back at the club. Who was I? What I didn't think was that my best friend from childhood would be at the other end of the stick. Shit was real fucking foul.

"Bitch, that shit ain't hurt. Untie me so it can be a fair fight," I taunted her and she backed up. Her foot came crashing down on my face and I immediately felt my right eye start to close.

"That's enough, Kells. He said don't fucking touch her. Explain that shit!" the chick said and Kelly turned and smacked her. Whap!

"Bitch, don't fucking question me! I do what the fuck I want!" Kelly roared and grabbed the girl. Kelly stuck her tongue out and the girl opened her mouth, welcoming the kiss. I thought I was seeing things, but these bitches were on some whole other shit.

"You better get on board, Sari. You will be part of us pretty soon," Kelly said and I laughed.

"Yeah, you a pretty little thing. We're going to have so

much fun with you," the other bitch said and ran her hands down my legs. I started to kick and Kelly laughed.

"Yeah, bitch, in your wildest dreams!" I snapped and she smiled, walking over to me. She tried to lean down, but as soon as she got close, I head butted her, making her nose bleed in the process. I smiled and she drew back and hit me again. This time, the chick pulled her away. She started to aid Kelly's bleeding nose as they walked up the stairs.

"He is coming for me! Jersey is coming, bitch, and you better be long fuckin' gone!" I yelled and tried to yank the chains on my wrists. It didn't do shit but hurt my already bleeding wrists. I prayed that Jersey or somebody had this location. I'd read so many books about females getting kidnapped and never returning, but I prayed my story wouldn't end like that. I started to silently cry, praying to God something happened. I knew bitches that went missing nowadays didn't get saved. Once you were gone, you were done for. I knew that wasn't the case for me. God had put me through too much for my life to just end here. I had to have a happy ending somewhere.

CHAPTER 8
Diamond

"You look good, ma," Fats said as I put my necklace on. I blushed and stood tall.

Smoothing my dress down, I looked at my reflection in the mirror. The girl staring back you wouldn't be able to notice the negative shit that went on in my head. I was suffering so easily. I had so much on my mind, I didn't even know where to start fixing myself and my problems. I wanted my pops here to tell me if I was doing it the right way. I wanted to avenge his death and get justice for myself but I couldn't do that so easily. I didn't know shit about the streets. Anything I knew now was from Sasha and her teachings. I was grateful for her because she had literally put me on. She taught me shit I would have never learned! Shit, like I've said before, I owe her so much! Without her, I wouldn't even be able to rock this expensive ass dress or these high ass heels I was wearing.

Checking myself out, I looked damn good. Eatable if I do say so myself! I knew I looked great because Fats couldn't keep his eyes off me as I moved around the hotel, getting myself together.

Fats was so motherfucking gorgeous. I never called niggas

gorgeous but he was so fucking beautiful. Standing at about 6'5, he had a goatee, which I was pretty sure he had just started growing out. His dreads were shoulder length, freshly done, and twisted into plaits. He had a deep dimple on each cheek, and though his lips weren't all that big, the way he licked them every time he talked made me want to suck on them.

Speaking of every time he talked... it should be a sin how white his teeth were. I thought they were fake at first. I could tell he wasn't a dirty nigga. The first time I saw him, even though he was dressed down, he still smelled good and clean. The way he talked, the way he walked, he was something special.

Right now, he was dressed up, standing next to me, and we looked like a motherfucking power couple. Fats wore a black and white Versace checked blazer with a black button-down underneath. He wore black slacks that stopped at his ankles, and black and silver Christian Louboutin Colonnaki flat loafers. If you were a nigga of caliber, you'd know them bitches run about a band or better. The only way I knew was because Jewel had just copped the same pair a few days ago. Let's not even talk about his jewelry. He had a diamond encrusted Patek watch. I stayed on Instagram and saw how the rappers flexed and this nigga's jewelry was on that type of status. He put that shit on and had me dizzy from all the ice he was rocking. He knew he looked good because as I was checking him out, he had the cockiest grin on his face, making me smile. When I think of a top-tier nigga, this was who I thought of immediately. Spectacular.

"Fats, go ahead, making my girl nervous and shit on her first hit!" Nova said, coming into the room fully dressed.

Rhythm, Valentina, and Treasure were already gone to the party. They were waiting for us to come and get it started. Queen was waiting at the airstrip, because as soon as we took care of business, we were going straight to the plane and going home.

"Thank you." I finally responded to his comment. Putting a strand of hair behind my ear, I was ready to get this shit over with. I didn't know why my nerves were so bad, but they were everywhere now.

"You do look good," Nova said, biting her lip and I blushed again. I did look good. I had on a red, strapless, floor-length gown with a slit that came up my thigh. On my feet were nude "So Kate" Christian Louboutin and I had a nude clutch to match. This was the first time I'd dressed up since I'd been home. Let's just say I wanted to get dressed like this every day. Nova made sure my makeup and hair were in place and we left out.

"When we get in, you just make sure you keep walking while I get us checked in. They won't search you, and if they do, I'll make a scene," Nova said and I nodded. I taped both pistols to my inner thighs like I'd been taught.

"Y'all got forty-five minutes and I'm coming in blazing," Fats said and I giggled.

"Nigga, don't get us murked. We are on somebody else's territory," Nova said and he laughed.

"Yeah, I'm tweaking. Just be out in an hour," he said and turned the radio up. My thoughts went to Sasha and my pops. I shook him out of my head and leaned back and closed my eyes. Shit was getting so crazy. I had stepped out of the prison field and into the streets. I didn't think my life would turn wild like it had. I was getting deeper and deeper into this street shit when I only wanted to come home and find out why my stepmom had done what she'd done to me.

"You good, Diamond?" Nova said and I nodded.

"I'm good," I reassured and she turned around. We were about to pull up to the mansion where Auk Latome was having the most talked about wedding reception in history.

She was also the princess of her city. Auk had married into a wealthier family who imported valuable merchandise to Sasha and her team. Well, somebody who was more powerful and ruthless than Auk put some tags on her, her three sisters, and mother. I guess they didn't want the heat to come back on them, so they hired us and we were here to collect.

Pulling up to the estate that the after-party was at, I stared in awe. This place was royalty, for real. Golden steel gates, a wide driveway filled with expensive ass cars I didn't even know they had in Africa, and a big-ass water fountain in the middle of the driveway; the house was something from a movie! You didn't see these types of houses in real life. I knew I never had.

The car came to a stop and my door was opened first. A guy with a clipboard held his hand out for my hand.

"Name?" he asked. I looked at Nova and she nodded.

"I was just in there... Name is Neko Mondesi," I said and he nodded and let me go. After Nova gave her name, we walked to the double doors where there was a line. After the five people in front of us went through the guards, I walked in with them. They stopped Nova at the door just like she predicted and searched her. I stood to the side and waited for her.

"Easy peasy," she said and smiled. Nova was rocking the same dress as me. Hair style the same and everything. When I looked around the room, I easily found Valentina and Treasure.

"They are about to make their grand entrance, come on," Nova said and handed me a champagne glass. I put it to my lips and didn't take a sip. I wasn't big on drinking and wanted to stay sober anyway. I would drink when we got back on the plane out of here.

The doors opened and two people holding hands walked out. I saw the princess and her husband. After a while of scanning the room, I saw her sisters and mother also. They were heavily guarded but I saw Treasure going in and out of the section that was roped off.

"Let's get this ball rolling," I whispered to myself and headed to the middle of the floor. Nova went to her side and nodded at me before turning her attention to somewhere else. Before I could even make it to my mark, I was grabbed from the back. One hand went around my neck, the other around my mouth as I was discreetly dragged to a back room. I looked around for my sister or even Nova, but I knew they were too focused on what they had to do to worry about me.

I was thrown to the ground and kicked in the side, making me croak and start coughing. I struggled to my knees, but the next hit knocked me down as I felt kicks rain down on me. I grabbed the first foot and pulled the blade from the inside of my jaw and started to swing wildly.

"Ah!" I screamed as I was grabbed by the hair and brought to my feet. The lights flashed on and I was brought face to face with the last person I wanted to see.

"Hello, Diamond," my wicked stepmother Alicia said and stood back, smiling. I tried to lunge forward but I was thrown back and hit in the stomach again. My eyes started to water because I wanted to kill her so bad, but I knew I was in a fucked-up spot right now.

"I just knew Sasha was going to send you on this hit... She's so fucking predictable. Like I don't fucking know she took my son!" Alicia screamed and reached back and rocked me. I felt dizzy and tasted blood in my mouth. I laughed because Alicia started to cry.

"Where the fuck is my son?" Alicia screamed and I spat in her face.

"Let me go and fight," I spat and she laughed. She nodded and the hands that were holding me up dropped me to the ground. I kicked the only heel I had on and got into a fighting stance. Before I could throw a punch, gunshots rang out and that was my chance to reach for the pistol I had taped to my thigh.

Letting off three shots, I ran to the door and bust it open. I spotted Treasure at the top of the stairs, going towards the main entrance of the hall. I immediately started shooting that way, too. No questions asked. Hitting the queen first, then the princess, I ran towards the stairs with Alicia's man on my ass. Tripping over the gown, I stumbled backward. Fats came out of nowhere, blasting, hitting one of Alicia's men in the dome. He grabbed me up by the arm as we hit the top of the stairs and Nova came out of nowhere with Queen, Rhythm, and Valentina.

"Let's go!" Nova screamed as we hit the door. The car was waiting on us and we hopped in and drove away as the other partygoers drove away in a hurry, too.

"Where the fuck was you at!" Nova asked, out of breath, as we got away from the scene. My adrenaline was rushing, and my mind was everywhere. I had just taken out two out of the five people on the list and was this close to Alicia's shiesty ass.

"Bitch, she was there!" I was finally able to speak. The whole car got quiet, and Nova kept looking at me through the rearview mirror.

"Who was there?" she asked and I sighed. I turned so she could look at me and I saw she was finally taking in my face and appearance. My dress was ripped, my hair was everywhere, and my jewelry was no longer on. I knew for a fact my face was bruised and swollen from the way Alicia's crew had fucked me up.

"If y'all wouldn't have started shooting, that bitch was going to kill me," I spat, thinking about how that bitch had caught me slipping.

"Alicia?" Treasure asked and I nodded. All of us were back in the car, heading to the airport, and I couldn't wait to be back home.

"Yes, I need some shit in motion, NOW!" I yelled and leaned back. I had nothing else to say. I knew shit was about to get ugly, especially with Alicia knowing we'd taken her son. All the shit she'd taken from me, FUCK HER SON! The bitch's life was on the line and she was worried about her maggot ass son! He wasn't going to be found, and pretty soon, she was going to meet that nigga in hell. I was going to make sure of that!

* * *

"How are you feeling?" Sasha asked, sitting at the edge of my bed. I sat up. I'd been in a real sour mood since the run-in with Alicia. No cap, seeing her in the flesh put me in a bad ass headspace. I just wanted her to die, and now. I'd never wished death on somebody as bad as I wished it on her. I know that shit ain't right, but the bitch had made her bed. Sasha said wait. Sasha wanted a concrete plan. Sasha called the shots. Sasha was going to have to hurry the fuck up with whatever she had planned because Alicia and her bitch ass son's days were numbered. I was sick and tired of waiting on Sasha!

"I'm good, I'm just trying to figure out what's next. We did the hit; what's taking so long for us to get at her? She still walking 'round free like she ain't take my pops, send me up the road, and fuck my life up," I asked, standing.

"Listen, with ya daddy being dead and you being locked up, he left some money to her. I'm waiting on my lawyer to find a flaw in the paperwork. I wanna take everything from here first," Sasha said and I laughed. I shook my head, not agreeing with shit she just said.

"Listen, I don't care about any of that. I don't care about you having these extra motives. She's gotta die soon. I came here because I thought you could help me. I've been out for six months and all I've been doing is contributing to YOUR organization!" I spat and Sasha stood up.

"All these motherfucking promises you made. I'ma help you do this. I'll help you do that! You ain't help me do shit! All the fuck you been doing is ordering me around, putting me there, training me to do this! I don't wanna do any of this shit! I don't even wanna fucking be here! I don't know you! You gave me up!" I yelled. Sasha just stood there with her hands crossed in front of her, letting me talk my shit.

"You spitting this hot shit about wanting to take everything from her, LOOK AROUND! You doing pretty fucking good. What else do you need? Money ain't the fucking problem," I spat, getting so fucking fed up with this shit. I wasn't taking orders from Sasha anymore! If Sasha wanted something done, she needed to get in the field herself.

"Only thing you've helped me do is—"

Before I could finish my sentence, a hand came out of nowhere, slapping the fuck out of me.

"Have you lost yo' fucking mind, talking to my momma like you crazy?" Treasure came out of nowhere, yelling. She was about to swing again, but I was too fast and hit her with a two piece, dazing her. She stumbled but recovered fast and came back with a three piece. Jewel came out of nowhere and grabbed Treasure as she tried to run up.

"Nah, let 'em go. They've been wanting to do this," Sasha said, looking at her nails, unfazed by us fighting. Soon as Jewel let Treasure go, I ran up and started pouncing on her. She did some type of move and made me fall back and got on top of me. Giving me a three piece to the face, Treasure put her knees on my arms and held me down. As she gave me two more hits to the face, I felt the blood in my mouth.

"BITCH, GET THE FUCK OFF ME!" I yelled and she smiled and blew a kiss at me. With all my energy, I flipped her off me and got on top of her. I started hitting her in the face and head, wherever I could hit. I grabbed her hair and stood up. This bitch had so much energy because, in one swift motion, she kicked me in the stomach, making me fall back next to my bed.

Treasure stood, grabbed her pistol, and cocked it back at the same time as I grabbed my pistol from under the bed. She was too fast, though. Her shit was already aimed at my head and mine was to my side, finger on the trigger, itching to bust it.

"ALRIGHT, THAT'S E-FUCKING-NOUGH!" Sasha yelled and I dropped the pistol and walked off.

"Fuck this shit," I spat as Jewel called my name. As soon as I made it to the front door and opened it, Fats was about to knock.

"What's up, bro?" Jewel questioned and Fats just stood, looking at me.

"Shit, I came for her." He pointed at me and Jewel laughed.

"Nah, that ain't happening and I told you my sisters were off limits!" Jewel spat and I laughed.

"Nigga, you ain't even know she was yo' sister. Man, chill out," Fats said and Jewel nodded.

"Let me holla at you," Jewel spat and he and Fats walked away. I grabbed my keys off the table and left. Fuck them, fuck this house, and fuck what they talking about. I needed to vent. I needed my daddy right now.

CHAPTER 9

Judge

"HOW IN THE FUCK Y'ALL LET THAT NIGGA GET AWAY?" I yelled, looking at the camera inside Big Man's club. The shit kept replaying. June stood there, shaking his head and Dolla wasn't anywhere to be found. This nigga had been disappearing lately. I ain't wanna think the nigga was on some foul shit because that nigga had shown how loyal he was a thousand and one times but the disappearing act was suspicious. I saw Lacy place something on the table in front of Asari and Asari took a picture. Just as the door opened, Lacy walked in and my phone rang for the millionth time with a notification. Ignoring all the texts from the crew, I saw a message from Asari and smiled when I saw the address.

"I had just gave her the address of the nigga who took her," Lacy said and slid me the paper. I nodded and handed my phone to June.

"Call the crew! We are about to make a long drive," I said and handed Lacy the wad of money in my pocket.

"If you see that nigga..." I stopped talking when I saw Asari turn around and hit a chick. I turned to June and showed him the screen. His jaw flinched and I saw his eyes turn. His baby momma was siding with the opps, had abandoned the kid, and broke his heart. He was a wild nigga before so she was only turning him up.

"This bitch gon' die," he spat and kicked the chair before storming out with my phone to his ear and his in his hand.

"If you see either of these bitches, hit me," I said and scribbled my number down.

"Take this. I'ma get at you as soon as I can," I said and jumped up to follow June. My first stop was to this nigga's house to get my girl. Then I was going to make sure everybody that even held a conversation with this nigga was dead. They all had to die!

* * *

"You got a picture of the nigga or something?" Bird asked, which immediately annoyed the fuck out of me. I had to take a second look at this fool and lean my seat back to get comfortable.

"Nigga, so this whole time you've been chasing a ghost?" I asked, trying to figure out why this nigga needed a picture of Tez. I wasn't up for the games right now. My girl had been gone for a few hours and shit wasn't moving fast enough for me. I had to hit up my boy Jah from up north to send some of his hittas. Yeah, I had hittas, but with the war we'd started and all the bloodshed, I needed to beef up security. My dukes and Bird's wife needed twenty-four-hour security, especially with us being in the streets real heavy. It was crazy because most niggas were scared to go to war with us. We had made a name a long time ago that held niggas in place. I didn't know what this old nigga's agenda was but shit was giving me obsessed vibes. He was infatuated with me or my brother's lifestyle. I couldn't see what his point was in coming so hard. Yeah, we had taken one of his but the bitch boy shouldn't have been trying to steal! He had to die and any nigga that thought they was going to steal from me would meet the same fate. So now here we were. I had started a war trying to get at this nigga and he started some shit he couldn't win. He was going to find himself dead with his head cut off, fucking with me.

"Nigga, I don't know this nigga and have never seen this nigga, so yeah, I been torturing the city for a fucking ghost," he spat and I laughed. This nigga Bird had been on a rampage since his car was shot up. I didn't blame him, though. My calmness and laid-back demeanor had niggas thinking I was a bitch or something. Before this little situation, niggas wouldn't have even thought to go to war with us, so I wanted to see who he was, and what type of power this nigga had that made niggas want to drop their nuts to challenge me.

I was being real cocky and big-headed, but that was how shit was. The streets of Indianapolis had been so motherfucking quiet since I took over. "That nigga crazy, don't fuck with him," was whispered around this motherfucker. So call me motherfucking cocky to think niggas KNEW better than to go against me. I was fucked up when that nigga shot me, but he only turned the savage in me up. I was in rare form and Judge ain't taken likely to beef shit. I wanted to end the shit a long time ago, but dealing with other shit like the business and Asari had me way off my square. I couldn't go like that.

"Man, bro, you got a pic of this nigga?" I asked June as he checked his clip. I knew he was shitty as fuck about his bitch, but he'd get over it. Nigga had his first heartbreak and it had to be his baby momma. I shook my head because I would hate to have to murk Asari if I ever found out she was moving foul like Tish.

"Nah, Sis had the picture," he said and I shrugged. I looked at Dolla, who was in his head, but I didn't say shit. I was going to holla at my boy later. Right now, I needed to stay focused because I needed to find my shorty.

"This the address the nigga used for his card at the club. I got two more addresses for the nigga. I'm sorry, bro." I said the last sentence for June because his baby momma was caught up in this shit. Her mom's address was a known spot for him.

"The bitch dead to me," he spat but I could tell by his eyes he was more hurt than mad. He fell for a snake and there was no telling what the bitch had told the nigga about my brothers and me.

The rest of the ride was silent with only the sounds of cars passing. I was too busy in my thoughts, hoping Asari was good. I just prayed she was at the spot we were going to. I had a feeling shit was about to get real motherfucking messy and I hoped it wasn't any of my people whose blood was spilled.

As we pulled up to the crib, my adrenaline began to rush and I hopped out of the car as soon as Bird pulled to a stop. The house was set up on a dead end and there was only one way off the street and I knew what that meant. One way in and one way out. I tucked both my Glocks and grabbed my AR. I didn't want to go in guns blazing, scared as fuck they were going to try to kill Asari before I could get to her. I had June's homeboy, Switch, with us. He picked the lock and the door opened. The house was silent. The only noises we heard through the house were low moans. Smiling, I knew we had that nigga caught with his pants down. I pointed to Bird and his crew to check the kitchen and basement. June and Dolla followed me to the back where the moaning was coming from. I pushed the door open slowly and saw Tish on top of Kelly, riding her face. Asari was tied to a chair with tape around her mouth. She was completely naked, and you could tell they had been torturing my shorty. She had blood coming from her nails, her body had purple bruises all over, and her left eye was swollen. When she saw me, her tears started to fall. She started to squirm in the chair and that was when Tish finally looked up and screamed. Kelly pushed her off and was quickly met with a bullet to the middle of her head. I saw June move like lightning, grabbing Tish by the hair. He threw her to the floor and started to kick her. Dolla grabbed June but he raised his gun to Dolla while he stomped her out.

"Don't fucking touch me, nigga!" June spat and continued beating Tish's ass. I was against domestic violence and men putting their hands on females. I wanted the nigga to murk her dumb ass, though, but we needed information from her.

I took my jacket off and wrapped Asari up as I untied her. I pulled the tape from her mouth and she immediately jumped into my arms, holding me tight.

"I got you, shorty," I whispered and Bird came to the back. His face held wrinkles and he looked sick to his stomach.

"Empty, but check this out. He got a picture of Ma and her nigga," he said, holding a picture out.

"Nigga?" I said, observing the picture. I almost threw up. I handed the picture to June and he laughed angrily, grabbing Tish's hair.

"How we let this happen? Nobody ran a background check on this nigga?" I asked as June handed me the picture and I looked at my dukes' nigga. I shook my head and looked at Bird.

"What?" he said and started to look around. I didn't know what for. He grabbed two phones that were on the dresser in the room, and I grabbed Asari.

"Grab this bitch. I ain't done with her," June told his niggas and they grabbed Tish and I led them outside.

"We need to get to Ma, now," I said and slid into the back seat with Asari clinging to my side. I heard her sniffle and knew she was crying. The sun was finally rising, and I just wanted to get my girl to a doctor so they could check her out then home.

"It's okay, shorty. I got you," I told her as we drove off. I saw the niggas my homie Jah had sent to me set the house on fire before trailing us back to my dukes' crib.

"You good?" I asked June and he nodded and clenched his jaw. He started hitting the dashboard.

"If you can't..." Bird started to say but he decided not to say what we were all thinking. No matter how much love he had for Tish, shorty had made her bed and she had to pay the price. She went against the grain and set the pick on her own baby daddy and his people. Shorty didn't owe me any loyalty, but she owed that to June. When she started working with the enemy, she chose her side. I know he didn't want to do it to his baby momma, but either he did or I did and I didn't give a fuck. I was going to make sure shorty went out the worst way if it was up to me.

"Ma don't know who this nigga is," Bird said to himself. I shook my head and wrapped my arms tighter around Asari.

"I'ma get you checked out as soon as we get to my dukes. Yo' sisters going crazy, man," I said and Asari looked at me.

"What? Man, them little girls ain't little. They've been hitting the streets, trying to find yo' ass!" I said and she smiled through her tears.

"You saw this nigga before?" Bird asked and I shook my head no.

"Not with Ma! Nigga, I would've been murked buddy's ass in front of her!" I snapped and Bird shook his head. My thoughts were with my momma and something told me the day wasn't over. Some shit was about to jump off.

Reaching for my pistol, I set it on Asari's lap and pulled the AR next to me. Asari looked up and I kissed her forehead. I could feel her body relax in my arms and I savored the moment because shit was about to get more wicked. She was going to have to put her big girl panties back on because that nigga was still out there and I didn't trust anyone!

CHAPTER 10
Nova

"I knew I was going to find you here," I said and sat down next to my girl, Diamond. I had a fifth of D'usse in one hand and two blunts already rolled, ready for us to ease our minds. I had gone to her dukes' crib to give her half of the bread but they had told me what went down. If nobody knew her frustrations, I did. Shorty had so much fucked up shit happen in so little time; she was breaking slowly.

"It's crazy 'cause you know Fish right around the way," I said and she smiled and wiped her tears. I sighed and passed her the bottle after taking a sip.

"Bitch, we don't have time for tears, we are on a mission! Be fucking happy, friend," I said and shoulder bumped her.

"You out! You beat a murder, friend. Some motherfuckers don't come home from that," I told her straight up. I knew she missed her pops, but we had all lost people when we were locked down. The tears were not going to help today's task. She wanted one thing and that was okay... Me? I wanted money and freedom. I still had shit going on with the family business and that shit felt like I was still locked up. I hated it, but I loved it for selfish reasons.

"Damn, Nov, I ain't know yo' pops was dead," she said and looked at me with the meanest mug.

"What you mean? My pops ain't dead," I said and she laughed.

"Ex-fucking-actly! You can't fucking tell me how to feel or what I shouldn't or should do. I should be happy and the only person I know loved me is gone? After all the fucking lies, the betrayal... You don't know, Nova. My own momma didn't keep me! My pops lied. I've been raised by... by a bitch who sent me to the worst place on earth! Bro, you don't know how it is! You don't!" she yelled with tears pouring down her face.

"Be happy, friend," she mocked me and I felt like shit hearing her repeat what I had just said moments ago.

"Be fucking happy because I'm not locked up? When I came out and was immediately put into some type of fucking crime mob family mafia shit? I don't know the fucking half of the shit Sasha got her hands in. I killed two innocent people the other night. TWO!" she vented and I rubbed her shoulder.

"All I wanted was to hurt the people who hurt me! That's it. I didn't wanna join this shit. I don't wanna be a part of a new family. I wanted my life to go back to normal. I wanted my daddy to be here when I got out." She cried and put her head on my shoulder.

"I'm sorry, friend. I'm so sorry," I said sincerely and she just cried.

"It's okay to cry. Let it out," I told her truthfully. I had to remember Diamond wasn't raised how I was. I was taught to not cry, and never show emotions! My feelings were tucked far away, and I barely got into them. If I did, I was by myself. Diamond, on the other hand, she was dealt a pretty fucked up hand. Right now, she was unstable and vulnerable. I felt bad for my girl because she wasn't the type to get into this lifestyle. Don't get me wrong, it was in her blood but only by default.

Before she was released, I didn't know who her people

were but as soon as I got out, my father and uncle put me on game. They let me know who was who and what was what. The fact that Diamond's pops was that nigga and couldn't see what type of slime bitch his wife was let me know he was fucking with the grimiest of them all. That bitch had him fooled and eating out the palm of her hands. Soon as my bitch turned eighteen, she put a plan together to get my bitch out of the way to take everything he had and she did just that. Alicia was a snake, and I was going to help my girl get her peace back.

"You're right. I don't know... What I do know about is pain! We both going through some shit. I'm here for you, though! For better or worse," I said and she nodded and took a drink from the bottle.

"But guess what? We make everyday count! We are getting our peace back and moving far away from this bitch, somewhere on a beach with palm trees. I'm thinking somewhere in the islands," I said and took a puff of the blunt. I smiled big, thinking of someplace better than here. I wouldn't dare spend the rest of my life in this city. Depressing, gloomy Indianapolis wasn't the city I wanted to raise a family in. Death and heartache lingered in the air. Waking up and smelling the bloodshed in the air wasn't part of my retirement plans. Nope! I was taking my friend with me.

"I can see me now. On the beach sipping Yella outta pineapple faygo. That sounds good," Diamond said, and I started to laugh.

"You ain't drinking nobody's lean, bitch," I cracked and she sighed.

"I pranked out bad at the house." She was stressed and it was my turn to laugh.

"Yeah, Fats told me you spazzed and pulled out the glizzy on Treasure. He also said he and Jewel got into it," I told her and she looked at me.

"Not because of me, right?" she wondered and I gave her a knowing look.

"Now you know it was because of you. Fats has been sniffing under you since the first time he met you. I don't know why you are playing with him. He's a good guy," I told her and she smiled. I could tell she liked him, too.

"But the shit we did—"

"Girl, ain't nobody thinking about yo' ass! We were both caught up in the moment and shit. The head was good, but baby, I love me some dick," I told her and she laughed.

"Plus, my cousin fucks with you. He ain't ever chased after no chick, so yeah, I'ma let him have you." I joked about the last part, and we laughed.

"I'm so glad bitches are in a better mood," we heard from behind us, and Treasure came and sat next to Diamond.

"Are we good?" she asked Diamond and Diamond smiled and hugged her sister.

"Yeah, we're straight," she said and handed Treasure the blunt. We put two in the air in comfortable silence.

"You gotta teach me that one move, though," Diamond said and Treasure smiled and put her arm around Diamond's shoulder.

"This is the plan," Treasure said and I smiled.

"I feel where your frustration is coming from, especially with the old bitch knowing we were going to be at the ball! That shit was weird, and I was trying to figure out how the bitch even knew we were going to be there!" she stressed and handed the bottle to me.

"Anyways, she wants you so bad, right? We just gon' have her come to you. She wants you so bad, I'm putting on a big ass party for you. Yo' birthday coming up next week, right?" she asked and we laughed because my girl's birthday wasn't until two months from now.

"Nah, sis, my birthday in two months," Diamond said and Treasure smiled.

"Well, according to this invitation, yo' b-day party is next Friday." She smirked and I laughed.

"Do Boss know about this?" I asked and she sighed.

"Nah, but it is what it is. We gon' handle it. Sis, you tired of waiting so we gon' get this over with so yo' mind can be at ease," Treasure said and Diamond nodded.

"I got my team and Jewel's boys ready. We need the big guns, though, so I'ma get Queen, the Wayne sisters, and Rabbit. I need you to get the rest of the girls on board. All this shit needs to be as clean as possible with Ma not knowing," Tres said and I sighed.

"Well, baby, we need to leave Rabbit's ass at home with that crazy-ass nigga and them crazy-ass kids!" I said and laughed at my homegirl. It wasn't a secret what we were into, but we were a team full of bitches. We had three different classes. We had us youngins, which consisted of myself, Treasure, Pandora, and Nautty. We were the youngins because we had under five years with the organization. We were the youngins but we were the ones who put in the most work nowadays. Nautty's ass been on her six-week post-partum let that nigga Fame pop her up the first chance he got. Pandora had just gotten her little jit back from her baby daddy, so she had been on mommy duties these past few weeks. Treasure and I had been in the field night and day. The middle class, we call them sister-wives. Nah, they weren't fucking the same niggas but those were the Wayne/Mayweather sisters. Y'all might've read about them ruthless bitches before; they had their own story to tell. They consist of four sisters: Rhythm, Melody, Harmony, and Lyric. They were some crazy-ass, ruthless females. They joined the team right after my pops did. They had their own shit going on with The Company, but their husbands took over. Now they were part of Queenz. The

OGs, Valentina, Queen, Princess, Sasha, and Meek were who y'all didn't want to fuck with. Sasha was barely in the field nowadays, but the other bitches? Listen, they were cutthroat Queen bitches from the trenches. They were so fucking raw and cutthroat, they had most niggas scared. They bust their guns with the niggas and were even in the field with most of the niggas who raised us youngins. Let's just say when Sasha started Headshot Queenz, she started a fucking genius ass organization. She cliqued up with Lady Nature once Valentina went Fed. They shut that shit down, and once V did her twelve-year bid, she came back to us and had been with us since. Y'all gon' learn about all these bitches I named in due time. Y'all know Miss Tina B. got some heat on the way.

Anyway, our shit was thorough! We had a clique full of tough, raw-ass bitches who loved to get their hands dirty. I didn't understand why Treasure thought Sasha wasn't going to know about this. Having every female with Queenz under the same roof was going to end with hella fucking bloodshed, so I hoped the plan to bring Alicia out was going to work because, if not, I felt bad for any innocent bystander.

"This ain't just a kill plan; this is also a meeting so Sis can meet everybody on the team," Treasure said and I nodded.

"So I'ma get my team together. You get the Wayne sisters and I'ma have Queen get the other ladies on the plan and we gon' get some shit in motion," Treasure said and we all stood. Diamond poured the little bit of D'usse we had out on her pops' grave and we followed Treasure to her car.

"In the meantime, let's go spend this five hunnit tho'," she cheered and threw two bags towards our feet. I smiled and bent down to look at my cut from the hit. I pulled three stacks out of the bag and handed them to Diamond.

"Nah, I can't take that." She declined and I smiled.

"Bitch, you put down two bodies. You earned it," I said

and she smirked and took the money. She opened her bag and her eyes lit up.

"Bitch!" she wowed and rubbed her hands over the neatly placed stacks.

"Let's go." She cheered and picked the bag up.

"Y'all go, I got some shit I need to handle." I was stressed and put my bag on my shoulder.

"I'ma slide later on tonight. You bitches better cop me something," I called out as I walked to my car. I waved to them as I drove to my destination. I grabbed my phone and had six missed calls from my pops. I sighed and cut my phone off. I didn't need any distractions with what I was about to do or else I was going to want to turn around and I needed to do this shit. It was crazy because as much dirt as I did in the streets, and blood I had on my hands, I was terrified to even bring this shit up. There wasn't shit I was scared of but this.

Being out for the past few months had been a blur to me. I was supposed to get out and stay out of the way. I wasn't supposed to be back in this life, but shit changed the moment my feet hit the streets. I vowed to God to get my shit together and I had failed miserably. I had to get my shit together because God wasn't going to accept a person like me in heaven if I couldn't even do right by my own family.

After thirty minutes of crying and driving, I finally pulled up to my spot. I sighed and grabbed a wipe out of my glove compartment. After wiping my face and putting my hair into a messy bun, I grabbed the duffle bag and got out of the car. I didn't even notice anyone sitting on the porch, but once I walked further into the yard, I was stopped mid-step.

"MOMMY!" my twin boys, Nassir and Nas, screamed. I stopped and couldn't believe they knew me or remembered me, I should say. They were some big ten-year-olds and I couldn't help but get on my knees and hug them as tight as I could without smothering them.

"Mommy? Who are you two talking to?" I heard and looked up at the most genuine face I'd ever met in my life.

"Nova?" Ashley said and wiped her hands on her apron. Yeah, I know. Nova has kids? That shit still sounds crazy as hell to this day. Nobody but Ashley and their father, Nakeem, knew I had kids out here. I got pregnant when I was sixteen years old and Nakeem was eighteen years old. He ended up getting killed a week after I found out I was pregnant. That broke everything in me. If it wasn't for Ashley, Keem's mother, I wouldn't have these little ones right here. I had planned on getting an abortion, but Ashley reached out to me and I hid out at her house for the whole nine months. When I had them, I bonded with my sons for three days and left them with Ashley. Still, to this day, it fucked with me how I had done my sons. I was young, wild, and had just started working for my father. Having those babies didn't fit into my life at the time. Sad to say, I didn't start thinking about my sons until I got locked up. I never wanted to see them, though, especially while I was locked down. I couldn't face them, knowing I had just said fuck them and gave them away like that. Ashley didn't see it like that. She made sure that whenever I was ready, I could come see them and get them back. Ashley always kept me in the loop with them, sending letters every week. She even made sure I sent pictures home every chance I could, just so they could know what their mother looked like. Like I said, she was the most genuine person I'd ever had in my life.

The tears I thought I'd cried out on the way here resurfaced and I couldn't wipe them fast enough without some sliding down my cheek.

"Ma?" I choked and she put her hands over her mouth.

"Look, mama, it's my mommy," Nasir said and I stood up and hugged Ashley as we both cried.

"Heffa, you've been out! You should've come and seen

me." She pushed me back and Nasir and Nas ran to me again, hugging me.

"I know, Ma. I've been..." I didn't have an excuse, so I just put my head down and she tilted my head back up.

"Don't do that. You are too beautiful for that head to be held low," she told me and grabbed my hand.

"Come on, boys. Let's show Mommy the house," Ashley said and they jumped up and down and fought to hold my other hand. I laughed as we went into the house. After Nas and Naseem showed me their rooms and the rest of the house, Ashley sent them to their rooms to clean up while we talked privately.

"What's up? What's been going on with you?" she asked as she poured me a cup of the tea she had been brewing on the stove. I sipped it and smiled, taking in the peppermint taste. I swear some things never got old.

"I'm really just now getting the time. In my head space been fucked up. My pops brought me back to do the same fucked up shit I'd been doing." I sighed and she shook her head.

"So what?" she asked and I put my head in my hands. Ashley knew everything about me. When I was with her those nine months, we got closer than close. She was the mother I didn't have, so yeah, there weren't any secrets with me. She was my savior. I loved her dearly and with my whole heart. Shit, it had been ten years since Nakeem was killed and I still loved and missed him so much.

"I'm doing one more hit for Queenz then I'm out. I gotta get far away from here," I told her truthfully and she set the cup down. It wasn't no secret with what I had my hands in, especially with Ashley. She knew what type of life I lived since I was sixteen years old and she accepted me for me and loved me no less!

"Okay, and?" she asked, knowing there was more to it.

"I want my sons. I want you and them to come with me," I said and she sighed.

"Don't... Don't give me an answer now. I was thinking maybe Hawaii," I said all in one breath and she just looked at me.

"I have enough money to start all of us over. We won't ever have to work again in our lives. I need you. I need them," I said and grabbed her hands.

"Nov, that's a huge decision to make. The boys are in school, I'm still working at the hospital... I mean, this house..." she tried to say, but I wasn't letting up.

"I found good schools for them there. I'll even wait until they finish this year. We can rent the house out. This is a nice neighborhood, so I know somebody is going to grab it up fast. Fuck the hospital, you hate it there anyway," I said and she laughed.

"I'll give you some time to think about it," I said and stood.

"I need to stash this here," I said and slid the bag across the floor.

"Is it okay if I spend time with them?" I asked and she smacked her lips.

"Girl, please. Those are your kids! Go, they won't let you leave anyway." She smiled and shooed me away. I smiled as I walked slowly to the back where my boys were supposed to be cleaning up, but instead, they were playing. I stood in the doorway and watched them. I prayed this hit with Alicia went as planned because I planned on getting out of here as soon as this shit was over.

CHAPTER 11
Chase

"How Sis doing?" I asked little brother Jersey as we sat, waiting for our momma to pull up. We had been there for about three hours, waiting while my dukes took the twins and Ginger out to breakfast and shopping earlier. Jersey had called around and got somebody to come look at Star to make sure she was good. Yeah, she was fucked up and they had definitely done some damage but it wasn't life-threatening. She was upstairs laying down, waiting for her sisters to get back, too. That was all she talked about was getting to see them.

"She fucked up. She'll be straight, though. I got her," he said and I nodded. I scooted the bottle of Remy to him, and he took it straight to the head.

Jersey was sitting across from me, while Dolla was sitting on his side. June was on my side. I could tell Dolla had some shit going on because lately, he had been off his square. That wasn't like him. Even right now, the nigga wasn't saying too much.

"You good?" I asked Dolla and he nodded. His attention went from Jersey to me and then back to Jersey.

"I'm straight, bro, just got a lot of shit I'm dealing with,"

Dolla said and scooted his chair back as his phone started to ring.

"The nigga went in hiding. We damn near got his whole family together," June said and I ran my hands down my face. I was more frustrated than anything. When I got out of the streets, I made it known I didn't want to step back in. This shit had me going against everything I wanted away from. I was trying to be legit now and turn over a new leaf. I still had it in me, but like I said, that shit was behind me.

"What's up!" Jersey asked, feeling my energy. June sat up in his seat and looked at me.

"We wouldn't be going through all this bullshit if you would've deaded that shit way back! You had a chance to get at that nigga but you was playing around. Taking trips, being at the strip club every day. Nigga, you slacked, and now that bitch ass nigga got a few up on us! On you 'cause this shit falls on you," I spat and Jersey smirked.

"Hoe ass nigga, you just as much a part of the shit as me! You forgot he hit yo' spot first! You let that nigga disrespect yo' club and ain't bust a move so he stood on yo' bitch ass! You waited on me to come back before you even put shit in motion and you niggas still ain't bust y'all fucking move! I'm the one making moves, hitting the motherfucking streets, day, and night! Fuck you!" Jersey spat and stood up.

"Nigga, I slid the same motherfucking night! Niggas know not to play with me like that!" I spat and stood up once he started to round the table. I was about 200 pounds and a whole three feet up on this nigga, but he still stood up, ready for whatever. I laughed and stood back to take him in. This nigga was me in my younger days: stubborn and thought he knew everything. I had to learn the hard way, though, just like this nigga.

"Niggas play with you! They play on yo' name, not mine!" I spat and he smirked and nodded his head.

"Yeah, okay! The nigga ain't dead yet 'cause he hiding. That's it," Jersey spat and it was my turn to smirk.

"Yeah, now, 'cause a few months ago, the same nigga was out running the streets, happy, bragging about what he did and what he was going to do. You a bitch nigga!" I said just to get under his skin. I wanted Jersey to get mad. The nigga was getting soft. Some shit would've been handled the day he came back from out of town but he was so worried about his bitch and everything fucking else. Jersey had never been this soft!

As a little nigga, he was stepping on business. I was real confused why the nigga was letting this nigga stand on them. This nigga brought pressure to the city. Stopped little bro's money flow, inconvenienced his family, shot little bro, and took his bitch. Niggas were standing on my boy and I was tired of it.

"Fuck you, bitch ass nigga. I been moving the way I move 'cause I got too much to lose! Nigga, I'm doing all this alone. I've been applying pressure. The only one. You been trying start a family, nigga. That's all you focused on and being a momma's boy bitch! This nigga June been worried about his scandalous ass baby momma, fucking everybody, siding with the opps. Yeah, nigga, you need to figure out how you gon' handle her before I do!" Jersey spat and then looked at Dolla.

"You, nigga. You suspect as fuck! Disappearing, being nonchalant all the motherfucking time. Yeah, nigga, I don't trust yo' ass so forgive me if a nigga been focused on everything else. Nigga, I gotta worry about the business and not being run up on by the Feds. Yo' hot ass had shit so motherfucking messy when I came into the game, I had to fix yo' fuck ups on top of trying to get some legal shit together to invest my lil money in. I'm a beast in these streets! I was pooping shit for you, nigga, so don't ever come out yo' mouth with that tough shit. I ain't none of these niggas or the peon niggas in yo' clique," he spat and stood toe to toe with me. I smirked cockily because the nigga had to look up to me. I was two times his size and he wanted to stand up against me. I smiled and started to laugh but was caught off guard when he cocked back and swung once, making me stumble back. He rushed me and started hitting me in the ribs, stomach, or wherever his hits could connect. After catching my breath, I picked his little ass up and slammed him on the table. In one swift motion, this nigga had his gun drawn, pointed under my chin. In a chain reaction, June had his pistol out, aiming it at Jersey as Dolla had his out, aiming at June.

"Are you niggas done or what?" we heard and my dukes came in with bags. She shook her head, walking around the kitchen, setting bags down.

"What's so urgent that we had to stop what the fuck we were doing and come here to see all this?" she said and turned to the girls who had walked into the kitchen. Ginger walked to me and hugged me and Love and Loyalty walked to Jersey and hugged him.

"Asari upstairs," he said after fixing his clothes and mugging me. The twins ran towards the stairs and my dukes sighed.

"Ma, did you know this nigga..." I started to say.

"Ma, the nigga you been fucking with is that nigga Tez!" Jersey said and slapped the picture of the old nigga Tez and my dukes on the counter.

"Yeah, my boyfriend's name is Maurice Queentez Washington. What are you saying?" she asked and turned around, looking at us.

"Ma, the nigga that's been after us is him," I told her and she shook her head.

"Nah. You sure?" she asked, then looked at Jersey. The way she looked made me shake my head. Ever since my pops died, my dukes had been fucked up. It had been all about us, her sons. Now that she had finally moved on, her new nigga had to die. She was fucking the opps and nobody even knew. I had met the nigga twice and didn't even know so I knew she was hurt right now. Especially knowing the nigga was about to die soon.

"Yeah, the nigga a fucking opp and he gotta die," June spat and I laughed. He still had his gun in his hand and had murder in his eyes. My momma sighed and went to her drawer in her kitchen. She rummaged through a few papers and brought something back to me.

"This is the address. He left this here one day. I had a friend of mine run his name and it came back to his land," she said and I nodded. I slid it to Judge and he grabbed it up.

"Before you go, sit. I don't know what y'all got going in the streets, but I need to talk to y'all," she said and sat at the table. June was so in his he stood by the doorway while I sat next to dukes.

"This beef shit can't be squashed without more bloodshed?" Judge laughed and stood up.

"Ma, did you not hear ya son?" I asked and she looked at me.

"I did, loud and clear, but what I'm saying is—" she started to say but I shook my head.

"Nah, what you're saying isn't making sense! We just told you this nigga is involved in a lot of fuck shit and you asking us to pardon his life. Excuse my language, Ma, but that shit ain't happening. The nigga and his whole fucking family are dead," I spat and she hit the table.

"Dammit, Chase, don't fucking talk to me like that!" she yelled and Judge started to laugh.

"Real funny, man. This shit wack as fuck! You sitting there like you ready to choose that nigga over us! That nigga shot me and burnt my house down! That nigga killed Asari's whole fucking family!" Judge yelled and my dukes sat down, looking at Judge.

"I'm sorry… I…" she stuttered and then looked at me.

"I just don't want y'all to get hurt," she said and Judge sat down.

"Too late for all that. That nigga fucked us over bad. It ain't no sparing that. You shouldn't even think that," Judge said and walked away.

"Be ready to move out in an hour!" he yelled and walked away. June walked off and I shook my head and went to find my wife. Ginger was sitting in the kitchen at the bar, eating. Since my wife had found out she was with child, all she seemed to do was eat. I didn't mind, though, because my baby had her ass even fatter, and she had this glow about her.

"Come chill with me," I told her, picking up her plate and cup. She smiled and followed me into the front room. I set her food down in front of her and she sat on my lap as she ate.

"You good?" she wondered and I sighed. I was tired and wanted peace. I wanted nothing but to be able to enjoy my wife, our pregnancy, and life. Shit was always going on and that shit was tiring.

"I'm good. When all this shit is over, I want you to pick anywhere and we're going," I said and kissed her neck.

"Anywhere?" she clarified and I smiled.

"Yup, just pick a place and book the flight with my card," I said and she leaned back.

"I love you, my baby, and if you need me, you know I'm here," she said and kissed my lips.

"We are about to leave back out in a minute and I just wanna chill under you," I said and she looked at me.

"Why do I have this weird feeling?" she said and turned around to face me.

"Why don't you wait it out," she suggested and I shook my head.

"Nah, Judge ain't gon' wait and I ain't letting him go

without me," I told her and she nodded. I saw the worry on her face and kissed her lips.

"You know ya mans a fucking gorilla. I'm coming straight back to you," I said and she smiled and rubbed her stomach. It had just started to form a little pudge and I was happy. That meant my seed was growing perfectly.

"I'm glad y'all brought Asari back. That's all those girls kept talking about when we were gone," Ginger said and I nodded.

"Little bro isn't letting up. He wasn't coming back to face them without his ol' lady with him," I told her and she nodded.

"So, it's bad?" she wondered and I nodded. I'd had my fair share of street shit, but niggas had never dropped their nuts and came at me directly. Yeah, niggas may have played crazy with some skrilla or some shit, but they never brought it back to my crib or hit my brothers. Ginger knew that. She was here from day one and I think that was why she was scared for me now. She knew I was deep in the streets, but shit had never hit so close till now. I was ready, though. I wanted to get this nigga and whoever he knew out the way so motherfuckers could know we weren't the niggas to play with. I wanted the streets to fear us so we could go back to living comfortably.

"Well, I trust that you'll make it back to me safely so I'm not even going to worry myself," she said and sat next to me. She put her feet on my lap so I could massage them and she leaned her head back. Right now, it was peaceful. At this very moment, this was how I wanted to feel with my girl and our family forever.

CHAPTER 12
Dolla

"STOP CALLIN' MY MOTHERFUCKING PHONE!" I snapped and heard laughter on the other end. I looked down the hallway to make sure nobody was coming and dipped into the bathroom.

"I need to see you like now," my egg carrier said, and I groaned. This call was an every-fucking-day thing. She laid low for a while because my pops was on her ass for reasons I didn't care to know. They hated each other, and I stayed the fuck out of it. I didn't fuck with her for the way she did me. Not because of that nigga; I barely fucked with him nowadays. He had been moving sketchy as fuck. Both of them had been moving like they were my enemies and now it had me moving funny, which made my niggas look at me sideways.

I had never been on any fuck shit when it came down to my brothers, so them questioning me made me feel some type of way but not for long, though. With the bullshit that had been going on, I didn't blame them. Right now, niggas wanted them dead and I was moving funny, so they were just being cautious. Judge knew I'd lay anybody down about my boy. That was just how much love and loyalty I had for the nigga.

My dukes was on some other shit and my pops was siding with anybody to get close to my dukes. I didn't even know why the fuck he wanted her head so bad. Shit was weird and gave me "If I can't have you, nobody can" vibes the way he was gunning for her. The nigga only called me to ask had I seen or talked to her. I was so confused and caught up with this nigga, Tez, I didn't have the time to sit down and actually see what they wanted from me.

"Aye, bro, holla at me right quick," Judge said, knocking on the door. I hung up with my dukes and opened the door.

"Aye, we gon' handle that old nigga first thing in the morning. I'ma sit with Asari and make sure she coo'. You go get some rest," he said and we dapped up. He started to walk away and then stopped and looked at me.

"You good? I know the shit with ya dukes coming back fucking with ya head and all, but you seem distant," Judge said and I nodded.

"I'm good. I'm just ready to handle this nigga so we can get back to the money," I said and Judge nodded.

"A'ight, nigga. Love," he said and shook up again.

"Love," I said and headed to the door after saying my peace to everybody.

Getting in my truck, I headed to the inner city.

"I'm about to slide, come holla at me," I said and hung up the phone. I grabbed my pistol and put it on my lap. I was ready for whatever and never knew what I was walking into, fucking around with either one of my parents. It was crazy that I felt I had to watch my own back from the ones who brought me into this world. My pops was just as fucked up as my dukes but I fucked with him more because he didn't leave. He didn't give up on me and he for sure didn't forget about me. I don't think I could ever forgive her for leaving the way she did, only coming back every once in a while. Nah, that shit wasn't forgivable and she knew it, too.

Pulling up to my dukes' hotel, she was waiting for me at the front. She hopped in the passenger seat and I drove off before she could even shut the door all the way. I wasn't pleased to be in her presence, but I knew she would keep calling me if I didn't see her.

"What's up?" I asked and she sighed.

"Look, I came back to get you to come down there with me and run shit. I need somebody to take over what I built, and before I let a nigga that ain't part of me take over my shit, I was trying to get a blood member," she said and I laughed.

"I'm good on that. Next," I said and pulled into an empty parking lot.

"Ya pops ain't up to no good. He for sure ain't the nigga you think he is," she said and reached into her jacket, making me point my pistol at her head.

"Hold up, nigga," she screamed and pulled a folder from the inside of her jacket.

"Damn, nigga, you was going to kill me?" she asked and I smirked.

"You lived your life," I told her and shrugged. She sighed and handed me the folder. Flipping through the pictures, I damn near threw the fuck up at what she was showing me. My eyes had to be playing some type of sick-ass tricks on me. I knew my pops was a sick ass nigga but to see the shit she just showed me had me opening my door, throwing up what I ate last night.

"Yeah, the nigga is foul... There's more," she said and pulled her phone out. She clicked some shit and handed me the phone and I saw my pops come in view with some nigga whose back was turned to the camera.

"I paid a lot of fucking money for you to come back and do the job," I heard my pops say.

"Yeah, but you ain't tell me the nigga was Bird's boy. I

wouldn't have ever taken the hit," I heard somebody say, and my pops laughed.

"I don't give a fuck who boy he is. I want them all dead. You leave the mama for me," my pops said and the nigga sighed.

"The mama? What she got to do with anything?" another nigga said.

"I'ma handle my wife, she is the only one who knows, and I'ma handle Laura. Her sons won't let that happen so I need them out of the way first," my pops said and I shook my head.

"What about yo' son?" another nigga asked and my pops smacked his lips like a bitch.

"What about 'em? He riding for his boys," my pops said and my dukes cut the recording off.

"I'm forwarding this to yo' phone. Keep the pictures. You don't gotta answer me on the offer, but just know this is the only way I can step down," she said, which I didn't give a fuck about. My thoughts were on my pops and my dukes opened the door and got out. She had walked to a truck that I didn't even know was behind us. I drove off and sped to my pops' house. I was just trying to figure out how the nigga was going to turn on me. I was his fucking seed. I was his only seed, and the fact that this nigga basically gave the go for a motherfucker to kill me was baffling. I was sick to my stomach with the news I had found out and wanted answers.

Pulling up to my pops' house, all the lights were out and I hopped out of the car. I grabbed the key that was under the mat and let myself in. My pops wanted to be so hard, for real. This nigga didn't have any type of security. He was moving like he wasn't a snake ass nigga. The nigga kept a spare key under the mat like when I was a teen and still lived there. No security or alarm or nothing. I guess he thought like Judge. Niggas wasn't dumb enough to try him. I guess he met his match because he was about to meet his maker. Going up the steps, I stopped mid-stride when I heard grunts. It was early in the morning and the nigga was about to die in the pussy. The best way to catch a nigga was with his pants down. Y'all didn't know how many bodies I had caught from a nigga lacking behind a bitch. Pulling my strap out, I was about to open it when his ringing phone paralyzed me.

"Hold on, baby," he said and I heard shuffling.

"Yo?" he answered and put the shit on speaker.

"They found her. They found us. They got her," the voice said and my pops sighed.

"What do you mean, they found her? How?" my pops asked and I heard him smack something.

"Kelly died. My house is gone. Them niggas done took damn near my whole family. I can't do this shit anymore with you, C," I heard and knew it was that bitch ass nigga Tez.

"Man, shut the fuck up," my pops said slowly, and I heard grunting.

"Ugh. Meet me at the spot on Jefferson at three o'clock," my pops said, out of breath, and Tez said okay and hung up.

"Bend that shit over," I heard my pops say and kicked the door in.

"Don't motherfucking move," I gritted and shook my head when the bitch my nigga was fucking wasn't a bitch. Yeah, he had a wig on, but the strong facial features let me know that he was a nigga.

"Son," my pops said and shot the nigga he was fucking in the head.

"Dammit, son," he said and tried to move, but I aimed my pistol at him.

"Don't fucking move!" I spat and he looked at me with his hands up.

"You been plotting the whole motherfucking time?" I asked, but knew the answer. I damn near wanted to shed a tear behind the foul shit my pops was on. My whole life, this nigga instilled in me how loyalty was everything, how my dukes ain't want me, some shit about morals and word is bond but the whole time, the nigga wanted me and my crew dead. I was so fucking lost.

"Why?" I asked and he sat down on the bed. He slowly grabbed his cigarette and lit it. Taking a long pull, he looked at the dead nigga and I saw the tears in his eyes.

"Oh, you care about that fag?" I asked and he bit the inside of his jaw. He was pissed and I smirked.

"So, you were plotting to kill me and Judge this whole time?" I asked my pops and he shrugged.

"Just get it over with now, nigga, 'cause if you don't, I'ma make sure I get you!" he said and looked at his dead ass lover. I laughed because all these years, I didn't think my pops was on that type of time. No signs were there unless I was too dumb to see it. He had bitches over but none of them stayed long. He was already bringing different hoes in and out and it was fucking me up because he didn't even give a fuck right now. He wasn't in his feelings about me finding out he was siding with the opps. He was sad because I'd killed his fucking boyfriend.

"You wanna know why?" he asked and I didn't respond. He was going to explain anyway. He was trying to buy him some time, but little did he know, he wasn't leaving this room alive.

"I ain't too much care for ya boy. I wanted his momma dead. I knew if I killed her, he was going to eventually come after me and I didn't want that. I used Tez to get at him while I worked up a plan to get ya momma and Laura. Ya momma knows too much, son. I can't let it get out about this shit." He pointed to the dead nigga and rubbed his forehead.

"Ya mama came to me a few months ago and said if I didn't make you join her team, then she would expose me. Laura didn't do too much of anything. She just knew too much, and for that, she had to die. Tez was going to kill her, but with everything going on, she had slowed down with being around him because of her sons. So, if you kill me, Tez will only finish the job. He will take out you, ya crew, Laura and even…" Before he could finish, I silenced him with two dome shots and a chest shot. I grabbed his phone and walked out the same way I'd come in.

* * *

Walking into Judge's mama's crib, I nodded at the guards he had posted at the door. I had gone home and showered and couldn't sleep with everything my pops had told me. Some shit didn't make sense. Why go through all that to make sure nobody knew you like fucking fags? That shit ain't make no type of sense to me. I was so confused on that part and how the fuck my pops even knew Tez. Looking at the pictures, my pops and Tez knew each other back in the day, too, because there were some old-ass pictures of my pops talking to Tez, but he was just a kid. I couldn't wrap my mind around everything and that was why I was back here to see if Mama Laura could help me piece things together.

I walked to the kitchen as I heard laughing and leaned up against the door frame as Judge and Asari sat at the bar, eating, and talking. Asari still looked bad, but not as bad as when we found her earlier. She had bandages on her wrists and ankles, and her black eye was still swollen shut but she was still a pretty girl.

"Mhm, mhm." I cleared my throat and they both looked up. Asari immediately stood and put her head down, but Judge grabbed her hand. He said something to her but I couldn't make it out. I sighed and walked further into the kitchen.

"You still beautiful, sis," I said and tilted her head up. She smiled and sat back down. I looked at Judge and shook my head. My thoughts went back to my pops and I slid the folder my duke had given me to Judge.

"I had to do it, bro," I said, barely above a whisper. Judge immediately stood up and pulled his pistol out, aiming it at me. Asari jumped back and I put my head down.

"I took care of him," I said and Judge set the gun down. He walked over to me and pulled me into a brotherly hug, and I let the very few tears I was ever going to shed over that nigga out.

"Where...where did you get this picture from?" Asari said, getting our attention. She held up the picture of my pops and the nigga Tez from back in the day.

"My dukes. Why?" I asked, and Asari studied the picture and sat down. She looked at Judge and he went to her side and wrapped his arm around her shoulder.

"The night my parents... The night he killed my parents, I walked in on Tez fucking this nigga," she said and I sighed.

"And that's why the nigga Tez wanna kill you," I said. I explained to them everything I knew. After telling them what my pops had said, what the phone conversation was about, and what my dukes said, Laura, Bird, and June were now sitting with us. It was sick that everything me and my pops said, Laura corroborated. To make matters worse, the funeral Judge and I met at was the funeral for a nigga my pops was dealing with. I was more disgusted than anything. The nigga lived a double life and had been living like that since before I was even born. Ma Laura even said back in the day, there was word that he was fucking with all the young niggas, having sex with them just to put them on. Some sick ass shit was going through that nigga's head and I just sat there. I wished I had killed him a different way. I wanted him to suffer!

"So, Ma, this whole time you knew C was..." Bird said and looked at me.

"Yes, I knew, but who am I to tell that man's business? Whatever he preferred was on him," she said and I nodded.

"So you knew the nigga was fucking Tez, too?" Judge asked and her mouth dropped.

"Nah. Fuck no," she said and put her hand on her stomach.

"Yeah, I saw with my own eyes the night my parents were killed," Asari said and shook her head.

"All this because a bunch of faggots don't know how to live in they glory?" June asked, which made me laugh a little.

"Killed my whole family because I saw them," Asari said and wiped the tears. Judge rubbed her back and she cried into his chest.

"Good thing is, I got his location and he'll be there at five o'clock," I said and looked at my watch. "We got three hours, so hit them boys and we can discuss all this other stuff after," I said and Laura stood up. I could tell she was physically sick about the shit she'd just learned and I shook my head. This was some very disturbing shit and I hated my pops couldn't just be openly gay. He would rather kill any and everybody who knew about him than to just be open. Now that was some weird ass shit for you. Then my dukes had me right in the middle of the shit. Man, how did God end up giving me two fucked up ass parents?

CHAPTER 13
Asari

"How are you feeling, sis?" Loyalty peeped in the room and I sat up. She looked so scared to even talk to me and I hated that for us. I wanted my sister to forever feel like she could talk to me about anything! Shit, all we had was each other for real. That had been like that since we were kids. This shit hit different now, though. I was so tired and exhausted from life itself. To top it all off, the shit Dolla had just told us was mind-blowing. This nigga wanted me dead that bad because he was a homo thug. Some crazy movie shit! I just couldn't see a nigga going through all this, killing a whole fucking family, just so nobody would find out he was gay. That shit was weird and beyond me!

"I'm feeling better. Come," I said and scooted over so she could slide in next to me. She smiled and came to the side and got under the cover with me.

"I'm sorry, Sari, I didn't mean anything I said," she apologized and I nodded. I didn't fault my sister for blaming me for anything we've gone through. My sister spoke her mind and that was that! I loved them dearly and would lay my life on the line for them! So that little shit she said had me mad, but I didn't give a fuck! I made it back to them, that was all that mattered to me anyway. Yeah, the shit was my fault! My parents, aunty and sisters were gone because of something I saw. Then the fact that they wanted Mama Laura dead, too, when she had never told a soul what she knew. That was some freaky ass shit! I just kept thinking there has to be more than just this because it didn't make sense to me. These niggas had to be fighting some real deal demons to want everybody dead because they were gay. I couldn't think straight right now.

"Girl, it's okay. I'm not worried about that little shit," I said and looked up to the ceiling.

"I'm getting us out of here. I'm getting us our own house, getting us back on track. I'm going to college and y'all getting back to school. We need a new scene. Our own space," I told her and she laid back next to me.

"Is... Did he take you? The dude who killed..." Her voice trailed off and I nodded. I wanted to be completely honest with my sisters. On different occasions, they proved to me how they weren't the same little fourteen-year-old girls they were a few months ago. Shit, a lot had changed for them in this past year and I wanted to be as honest as possible.

"Yes, he did, Love," I said, barely above a whisper. My voice cracked and I quickly wiped the tears that fell. I didn't want to cry but I couldn't help it. I was just happy because I was back home. These weren't hurt tears; they were happy tears! I prayed daily that the Most High brought me back to Love and Loyalty. Shit, I even prayed to be back with Jersey.

"What... What did he do to you?" she asked, pulling the covers back. I was dressed down in a tank top, shorts, and a bonnet on. I sighed and stood up. I took the tank top and shorts off and stood naked. Pulling the bonnet off, Love gasped and stood up next to me. She ran her hands through my hair, touching the bald spot. Closing my eyes, it seemed like I relived the days again and again. Bald spots, knots, blood clots, bruises, and a few missing back teeth were it for me. I held my head high, though.

"Did... Did he rape you?" she whispered as she touched my arms and ran her hands down the bruises on my stomach. She silently cried as she looked at every bruise and bump on me. I sighed and stood back.

"Yes, he did," I whispered back, afraid to say the words out loud.

"Right before Jersey found me. It was only once," I said and cleared my throat. I was going to take that part to my grave. Grabbing me by the shoulder, she leaned into me and cried.

"I thought you were dead. What were but I knew I couldn't live without ever speaking on that. I fought as hard as I could not to let that nigga take my innocence away, but it didn't work like that. He starved me, beat me, and raped me. That was some shit I didn't want to think about. Who was I kidding? I lost my parents, three of my siblings, and my only aunty; that rape and abuse shit wasn't anything I couldn't handle. God gave His toughest battles to His strongest soldiers, and I knew I was strong as fuck with the shit I'd been facing my whole life!

Love sat on the bed and put her head in her hands. I slipped my clothes back on and sat next to her.

"I'm... I'm okay," I stuttered. I grabbed her we gonna do if you didn't come back?" She cried and hugged me tightly. I sighed and put my head on top of hers.

"Y'all smart. If anything ever happens to me, y'all gon' be straight. Before I go, I'ma make sure y'all straight forever. I'ma die trying to make sure y'all good! We lost everybody in our corner! EVERYBODY! We only got us! Jersey, Mama L... they can all change up today! They can put us out right now and be done with us but we still have each other. I'ma always have y'all and that's vice versa," I told her straight up and she wiped her tears.

"That nigga wanted to break me, Love. He wanted to break me down badly! I ain't let him, though. He took everything away from us, from me." I cried and sighed.

"This is some sick shit we are going through. Some shit I would never have imagined happening to me!" I told her honestly.

"I owe Jersey, though. While that nigga was making my life a living hell, in the process, Jersey took everything from him," I told her and she nodded. I wasn't going to get into details. I didn't know what all Jersey and his boys did in the streets, I just knew I'd heard Tez say a few times somebody in his family or clique was missing. I knew Jersey had caught up with them. I just wanted that nigga dead and I wanted to be the one who took Kelly off this earth, but I knew I couldn't handle her being my first body. Even though she was a snake and had betrayed me in the worst way, something in me still loved her.

"I love you, Sari," she said, and I hugged her tightly.

KNOCK! KNOCK! KNOCK!

Loyalty stuck her head in, and when she saw Love and I talking, she came in and sat on the other side of me.

"Is he dead?" she asked and I shook my head.

"Not yet but he will be soon," I said, and she sighed and sat back. She didn't respond, and we were just in our own thoughts. I don't know when I dozed off, but I was woken up by Jersey tapping me.

"Asari." He tapped me softly and I looked down and the whole bed was soaked, even his clothes.

"I'm..." I was about to say, and he helped me up.

"You good, ma. Come on." He grabbed my hand and we walked to the bathroom that was connected to the room. Jersey cut the shower on and helped me get undressed.

"You shower, I'll be right back," he said and grabbed some

cleaning stuff from under the bathroom sink. I stepped into the shower and let the water run over my whole body. I don't even know how it happened. I was so stuck in my nightmares; I didn't even feel the pee coming out. I was so embarrassed, I slid down the wall and started to cry.

"Nah, shorty, we good," he said and slid in behind me, pulling me onto his lap. I still hadn't told Jersey everything that happened, but he didn't pressure me, either. I was embarrassed, ashamed, and most of all, I was hurt. I just wanted my life to go back to how it was before Jersey and I got together. Before my sisters and aunty were dead. I wanted all this to go away.

It's okay, I got you," he whispered and I started to cry harder.

"I was raped Jersey. He raped me," I barely got out and felt his body tense. His grip around me tightened and he held me closer. Even though the water had run cold, he didn't care; he held me in his arms until I was all cried out.

Jersey stood up and carried me to the room. Wrapping the towel around my body and hair, he grabbed the oil and sat next to me.

"Tell me what happened. Everything," he said and grabbed my leg to oil it down.

"They... um..." I cleared my throat and looked at the floor. I sighed and felt the tears build up.

"Kelly said that he would make me part of them. He's obsessed with me, Jersey. She showed me videos of me dancing at the club. I never even knew the nigga was back in town. He had pictures and videos of me when I was younger and of me and my sisters," I told him and he looked at me.

"He was stalking me," I added, wiping my tears.

"He raped me, Jersey. After everything I've been through, I knew shit couldn't get worse... but he broke me." I cried and he stood up in front of me. Jersey pulled me up and wrapped his arms around me. He didn't respond, he just held me tightly and it made me cry more. I thought I was going to die there! He planned on killing me and I was just happy that Jersey found me before he could do that. My life had been a whole fucking movie. A sad-ass scary movie.

"You good now. I got you," he whispered and held me closer as I cried. I just wanted it all to be over with now. I didn't have any more fight in me! I was done completely.

CHAPTER 14
Diamond

"You look beautiful today," Fats said as he held the door open and I stepped out of his car. After a lot of convincing and begging, I finally let him take me on a date. My birthday was finally around the corner and I was more excited for this party Treasure was throwing me tomorrow. I had to push that to the back of my mind, though, because I wanted to actually enjoy my date with him.

Stepping into an upscale restaurant called Below Zero, Fats gave his name to the host. She directed us to a nearby elevator and we stepped on. Fats immediately wrapped his arm around my waist, pulling me close.

"You smell good," he said and kissed my neck. I blushed and looked at myself in the mirror inside the elevator.

"And you match my fly. Yeah, you a problem!" He smirked. Looking at us through the mirror, I pulled my phone out and snapped a few pictures of us. One would think we were a power couple that had been together for years, the way we complemented each other. I was rocking a long black, strapless dress that had a mid-thigh slit. It fit my body perfectly and the six-inch heels I had on made my legs look longer. I had gone to get my hair done in wild curls and had a professional beat my face. I had gone all out for this date and I didn't know why. Shit, yeah, I did; I was feeling Fats and I knew he was feeling me, too.

Just by the casual conversation we had previously, I learned he had one kid. A five-year-old daughter and his baby mother died behind some shit he had going on in the streets. I also learned he has two brothers and one sister. Fish was his sister, and I was glad that he didn't hold me responsible for the shit that happened with her.

Anyway, I was looking good and feeling good, too. The way he stared at me and licked his lips made me want to ride his face all night. Fuck dinner, let's go straight to dessert.

I don't know if it was the fact that I hadn't had male attention in a long fucking time, but every little thing this nigga did had me blushing and smiling. On top of him being fine as wine dressed up, I was horny as hell. My nigga was rocking a black and red

"I never saw how beautiful your smile was," he complimented, which made me smile more. The waiter escorted us to the rooftop and there was only one table up there. Taking in the whole view was amazing. I saw all of downtown Indianapolis, Indiana, and then some. The table was set up nicely with a lit candle in the middle. On the stand next to the table was a bucket of ice with two bottles of wine or champagne, one of the sort. I couldn't tell from the distance we were standing at.

"Right this way," the waitress said, coming to us with two menus in her hand. Once we reached the table, Fats pulled my chair out and I sat as he went to the other side and sat. Once she left us alone after making our drinks choices, I looked up to see Fats staring at me.

This man was so fucking sexy. He had his hair done in a style that had a bun at the top of his head. I thought it was the sexiest thing to know how well this nigga took care of himself. Every time I saw him, he was well put together, not a hair out of place. Jewelry was bussing and the way he rocked this black and white stripe Amari sweater with the matching pants had him looking like a fucking boss! On his feet were black and white Alexander McQueen loafers and I knew he was sitting on dough just by looking at his appearance.

"This is beautiful." I gushed at the city and he sipped his water.

"Yeah. The first time I saw it, I was amazed, too. Sometimes I make reservations for myself just to come watch the city like this alone," he told me and I nodded as I looked at him. He sat with his hands crossed on the table and I could tell that even though he was a street nigga, he had also been raised the right way and had class. Yeah, I love me a bourgeois nigga.

"Yeah, it's definitely a whole vibe out here," I said and he sat up straight, leaning into the table.

"So, what's good on the menu?" I asked and he glanced at it, then closed it and set it down.

"They have this steak and stuffed shell meal that's pretty good. What do you have a taste for?" he asked and I blushed. You. I got a taste for you and you only, baby.

"Uh, I'm not sure." I cleared my throat, and the waitress came back.

"Are you guys ready to order, or would you like a few more minutes?" she asked and Fats looked at me.

"I'll take the wrapped steak meal with garlic potatoes and grilled shrimp," Fats ordered and I closed my menu.

"I would like the seafood pasta," I said and handed the menu back. Fats nodded to the waitress and leaned back towards the table with his hands folded.

"So, tell me, what's ya plans now that you out?" he asked and I sighed. I didn't have any real plans. My first priority was getting to know my real family, but shit had changed now that

I was out. Sasha was never around so we hadn't spent too much time together. I could tell her focus was on her business and I wasn't trying to stand in the way of that.

I didn't have plans, though. I wanted to get back to life, but shit was so different. I didn't have a clue about getting my life back on track.

"To be honest, I don't have a plan. All I wanted was to come home, but now that I've been home, all I've been thinking about is getting my payback. Now that Treasure has put this plan together, I don't know how to feel… which leads me to ask… Why didn't any of y'all people make a move on her? She hired them to get at Fish and me," I asked and he sighed. I didn't want to bring Fish and that situation up and ruin the mood, but I still wanted to know. Nova told me how powerful her people were, but they hadn't made a move on Alicia and who she was working with. I didn't give a fuck about the ones who came at us. I wanted the head of the person that sent the hit.

"I ain't gon' lie to you 'cause it's some shit ya dukes must've ain't told you," he said.

"Ya pops owned a company that's bringing in millions on a daily. When he died, he left it to you, but you were locked up, and some kinda way, Big A got that shit signed over to her. Only way Sasha can get it back in your name is if you kill Big A. It's deeper than you even know. Like in this game if any of the heads—Sasha, my uncle, pops, anybody from Queenz or whoever else she fucked over—tried to get at her, the niggas she works for would wipe all of us out. You, on the other hand; you don't even know how powerful you are! You don't know who yo' pops really was! You're above all of us! Yo' pops was above all of them," he said, leaving me more confused than ever.

"Look, say we got a triangle. The top is the highest, the bottom is the lowest. Me, Jewel, and Treasure are at the bottom. Yeah, we run our own shit and we got niggas out here that work for us, but we still considered the lowest. In the middle it's Sasha, my pops, uncle, a few ladies from Queenz and a few other people. Then at the top was yo' pops. We all had to answer to him. He was the highest. He had a few niggas under him who gave word back to us but all that shit changed when Alicia killed yo' pops. She became head and the niggas that worked right under yo' pops, they became head, too. So now ya pops ain't the head, Alicia, and the niggas yo' pops used to have over Sasha nem is head. So, nah, we can't touch her, you got to! You are in charge by blood," he said and the wheels started to turn in my head. I was so confused.

"But... why Jewel or Treasure can't handle it?" I wondered and Fats laughed.

"Sasha raised them. As far as we all know, we only got her word that OG was they pops. Ain't no proof," he said and leaned back. He stared at me and I sighed.

"So I can just walk in and take over her shit right now," I said and he laughed.

"Shorty, she's running yo' shit for you. If you go to yo' pops' lawyer, he'll tell you everything you need to know," Fats told me and I nodded. I had so many questions, but the only person that could answer them was my pops. I needed to talk to Sasha badly because, at this point, she was going to tell me something!

"Okay, anyway... let's change the subject," I said and the waitress brought back some type of bread and salad.

"Thank you." I smiled at the waitress and she walked away.

"So, do you want kids?" he asked as he started to eat the salad. I nodded and took a sip of the wine.

"Yes, I do. Just not right now. I gotta get my life together. I don't even know where to start to pick up the pieces, to be honest," I said and he nodded.

"I'm here to help you, so whatever you need, just let me know," he reassured me and I smiled.

The rest of the dinner went well. We chopped it up all night about everything that came to mind. I found out more about him and his family, his relationship with Nova, and the dramatics with his baby momma. We also talked about my pops and the shit that happened while I was locked down. Conversation flowed naturally and I was happy shit didn't feel forced. I must say, if I had to rate this date, it would be a ten out of ten. He had me smitten in so little time. I was scared of what could possibly happen once shit went further than what it was.

* * *

"How dare y'all motherfuckers!" Sasha roared and threw the chair across the room. I wanted to laugh because she looked so fucking dumb, but I just sighed. I looked at Treasure and Nova and leaned back into my chair. Nobody said anything, but I was on the verge of snapping! She was going on and on about us making a plan for Alicia when that was her fucking job. When she got me out, she knew from the start what I wanted to do. Now that the plan was in motion, she wanted to be mad. Nah, that shit wasn't sliding with me.

"With all due respect, boss lady, this shit is well overdue," Nova said and Treasure sighed.

"You got something to say?" she turned and asked Treasure. I sighed even louder because I saw shit was about to go south.

"Look, either you give us your blessing in taking her out or we gon' do this shit without you. I don't know—"

"Yeah, you don't know, so I'm trying to figure out why any of y'all thought it was a good motherfucking idea to bring in the OGs of Queenz and put a plan together to take out Alicia.

If this shit gets back to the head team, the niggas that's over me, y'all Alicia. then all of us are dead. Y'all know that, right?" she asked and looked at every lady in the room.

"And we ready to go to war about ours!" the one I knew as Princess said. She smiled and so did I. I grabbed the bag I had at my feet and stood up.

"My pops left me with a lot of money. Shit gon' get real motherfucking serious tonight. She's coming for me and she's coming hard!" I said and Sasha sat down, shaking her head.

"Y'all don't even know me and know the consequences we are facing when we walk into this club tonight. So, for that, I'm forever grateful. I know this ain't a lot, but this is a million dollars to split between y'all ladies," I said and slid the bag into the middle of the table as best as I could. Treasure stood up and reached for the bag. She unzipped it and the bundles of money started to fall out.

"Nah, we doing this because you are one of us! Anytime anybody ever came at us wrong, Ma, you deaded that shit quick! A motherfucker crossed us, Ma, you was the first to ever take charge and we got at 'em! Now Sis has a problem and you tuck yo' tail! Yeah, some shit ain't adding up," Treasure spat and put her hands on her hips.

"So what you saying?" Sasha asked, standing back on her feet. I saw this going all the way south so I sighed and started to get in the middle of them.

"We know Sis gotta be the one to pull the trigger on Big A," Treasure said and Sasha sighed and looked at me.

"And I will!" I spat.

"Everybody out! Don't leave, just get the fuck out!" Sasha spat and everybody started to leave except Treasure and me.

"You out, too!" she told Treasure and Treasure sighed and walked out.

"Sit down, Diamond," she told me and pulled the seat next to me.

"Look, there's a lot of shit you don't know about me, yo' daddy and Alicia. The shit is way deeper than you could even imagine!" she said and I sat back and crossed my arms. I knew I owed Sasha so much respect for getting me out of prison, but I couldn't respect the way she had done me. I tried to have a good relationship with her off the strength of her coming when I needed her the most but that wasn't enough. I deserved a real mother, real love. All this time, I'd been raised by a woman who I thought was my mother, and the whole time she wasn't. On top of that, she treated me like shit! My whole life, I'd been mistreated all because she had family issues, so she said. I didn't even give a fuck why my pops raised me without her, but it still ate at me how shit played out. Treasure and Jewel were raised knowing my pops but I couldn't know my mother? Some shit didn't make sense in life and this was one of them.

"Look, yo' daddy started this shit from nothing. He brought in me, Alicia, and a few other top old heads. When I got pregnant with you, I stepped down. The old heads that worked with yo' pops stepped up and they became one. Yo' daddy didn't want me to come back into the game so I left you with him and moved to Ohio and started Queenz. I was young and wild. Shit, the streets was all I knew back then. I wasn't about to go legit when the fast money was so fucking easy to get. Yo' dad and I always kept in touch and shit but time flew past and you had forgotten about me. Then yo' daddy and I linked up one time and that was how Jewel was made. We came to a mutual agreement that I would keep Jewel. Yo' dad wanted to stay away, and he decided to keep me and you a part, but I always told my son who his father was. Then I came into town for a client and we linked again, and boom, Treasure was made. Yo' daddy and I always had a connection. He was my first and my last, we just couldn't get it right for us. For y'all!" she said and I sighed and scooted my chair back.

"Look, no disrespect—"

"Let me finish," she said lowly, clearing her throat. "When yo' daddy died, Alicia stepped in his place which means she's part of the old heads. It's too complicated to even explain." She sighed and leaned back.

"Okay, so this is how it works. It's five men; yo' pops is always number one. Then it's his top hitters. We know Alicia took yo' daddy's life but we don't have any proof 'cause the bitch is slick as hell. Brick is the main hitter and he has brothers. That's who yo' pops trusted the most with his whole fucking life. So when he died, the next person to step in was supposed to be you, but Alicia moved in, so the only way we can take Alicia out is for you to do it. And there can't be no word that my team had anything to do with it," Sasha said and I nodded. Jam, S but it's damn near too late for the truth. I got one thing on my mind and that's handlining what I gotta do! I let this shit sit on the back burner for too long! I'm just trying to figure out how you can sit down and take the shit..." I said, feeling myself getting pissed about everything.

"You wanna know why I haven't made a move on A?" Sasha asked and I nodded. Of course, I wanted to know. Shit, from what I'd learned, not only had Alicia fucked me over, she had killed my pops, took over their business and had also pushed Sasha out the way and was running some shit that belonged to Sasha! So yeah, I was so confused about why she was still alive.

"First of all, we don't have any type of proof that Alicia killed yo' daddy. It's so much shit you don't even know," Sasha said.

"So the shit you told me about my pops not knowing about Tres and Jewel was a lie?" I asked and she nodded slowly. She wouldn't even look me in the eyes. She knew she had done me wrong. I was so fucking mad at my pops and

Sasha. The two people who were supposed to protect me at all costs were the first to betray me.

"So you can't touch her, for whatever reason, I don't give no fucks about! She's dying! Tonight! You just choose what side you wanna be on," I spat and stood up. I was fed up with the conversation with Sasha and the shit she was saying! She wasn't making sense to me, and I hated to treat her this way, but she was seriously blowing it with me and we had nothing else to talk about.

CHAPTER 15
Judge

"Just don't go yet," Asari begged and I sighed. She looked much more relaxed than when we first brought her back here. I could tell she just wasn't ready for me to slide out, though.

The shit Asari told me she went through fucked me up bad. Man, I didn't even know how to help shorty get through the shit she'd just endured. I definitely didn't want to leave her right now, but I had to handle some shit. She didn't understand that, though. She needed me by her side, and I needed to get back to business. I wasn't sleeping until shit was handled.

"Jersey, please just stay for a little bit," she said and the tears she was holding finally fell. I sighed and leaned up against the door frame as she looked at me, pleading with her eyes for me to stay. For every tear that slid down my shorty's face, there would be a bullet sent into that bitch ass nigga. I had never seen my shorty cry the way she cried. The nightmares, the screams; that shit fucked my head up bad. My shorty was so fucked up, she pissed on herself behind that shit. I knew my girl was strong, but this shit right here had me looking at shorty like she was superwoman.

"Jersey... please," she whispered, then grabbed at my hand.

I wasn't being insensitive at all, I just wanted to go handle this shit, then make it back to my girl right away. With everything Dolla had found out and putting me up on that shit was wicked. Not only was my girl in the middle of this shit but they were trying to get at my dukes, too. I shook my head because the whole time my dukes was fucking around with this new nigga and didn't even know he was Tez! She was sleeping with the enemy the whole time.

Rubbing my hands down my face, I pulled Asari into my chest and held her tightly. I felt her body relax and held her tighter.

"I gotta go handle this," I said and kissed her forehead. Asari sighed heavily, then wrapped her arms around my waist.

"Come on, get back in bed." I ushered her through the house and she held my hand tightly. I promised after this shit was over, I was taking my girl and her sisters away from this shit. There were too many bad memories left in the city for us. We had to pick the pieces up somewhere else. My shorty was literally living in a nightmare, and there wasn't shit I could do. The words Bird spat at me were a reminder that I had failed my girl. I was supposed to protect her at all costs and because I was slacking, the nigga got too close to us! It let that nigga shoot me! All the hustling I was doing in these streets, a motherfucker never had the balls to come full throttle like that! This nigga had to go, and I was making it my mission to not let them breathe another day!

"I don't want you to leave right now," Asari whispered as she climbed into bed. I pulled the covers over her body and kissed her forehead.

"I got to. I'm coming right back, though," I told her and kissed her lips softly. She pulled me in tightly and kissed me again. I could tell she wanted to say more, but I got out of there before she could say anything else. It was almost time for us to meet at the spot Tez thought Corey was going to meet him at. The whole time, we needed to be there before him so we could scope shit out. I needed to handle anybody he had on his side. I needed this shit to be done tonight! I wasn't sleeping until I knew he was a fucking memory!

* * *

"So, go over this shit again," June snapped and leaned his seat back. He wasn't himself right now and had been in his feelings ever since he had to knock his baby mama off. She was a snake, and if he couldn't pull the trigger, I would have! The nigga Tez knew so much about us because of Tish and that was foul. She was the grimmest of them all and if I could, I would have brought the bitch back just to smoke her myself.

"Man, listen, this is some weird ass shit." Dolla shook his head and started over from the beginning again. He had to tell the story again and again and that shit still didn't make any fucking sense. To know this weird ass nigga only wanted my girl because he was a faggot was comical. Then to know the nigga C was in on the shit had me looking at everybody sideways. Dolla's pops, Corey, and my dukes were real close, so to hear he wanted my mama dead too was sick. I felt bad for my nigga for having to smoke his own pops, but like I said before, if he wouldn't, I would! That nigga didn't deserve to die so easy, though. He was supposed to get tortured! He had the easiest death and that shit had me hot!

"We got the team in place. It's about time," Bird said and grabbed his Glock. We were all strapped but I wanted to be the one to end this nigga. I wanted the kill shot. As soon as I checked my clips, lights came from down the dark road and I knew it was the nigga Tez. I didn't see any other cars behind him and smiled. This nigga was moving with no hitters, like he hadn't come to my city to try to turn it upside down. Nah, fuck that! He turned this motherfucker upside down. Murder rate went up and the streets went dry. Yeah, his time had expired.

Then the shit with my boy's pops had me disgusted, for real. As long as I'd been around OG, I didn't have the slightest idea he was on that. I knew my boy was fucked up having to take his pops' life so I didn't even want to ask my nigga how he was feeling because I knew that shit was eating him up. Especially knowing your own flesh and blood were plotting to kill you and your niggas.

"This nigga crazy," Bird mumbled, probably thinking the same thing I was thinking. As the car pulled across the way from where we parked, he got out with three other niggas. They started walking towards the entrance of the abandoned building Corey was supposed to be waiting at. This nigga thought he was so motherfucking untouchable, rolling with two niggas and walking like he owned the city.

I was the first to open my door slowly and my crew fell behind me. As soon as I got close enough, I aimed and hit Tez twice. Once in the back and once barely hitting his neck. That made him fall and one of his niggas quickly grabbed him up, while the other let out shots towards me and my crew.

Running after them, they ran inside the warehouse and I kicked the door that had shut and they started shooting our way. Bird waved for his crew who was outside, waiting for the signal, and they rushed inside. Tez's crew was dropping Bird's niggas but I ducked behind the first thing I saw and fired back. I saw Dolla and Bird run after the other two niggas who came with Tez so I took off after them. Dolla hit one nigga and I aimed and hit the other nigga that Bird was chasing. Walking up on them, I shook my head because the little nigga was one of the twins' little boyfriends, who Dolla had to get on one day.

"Kill me, pussy, 'cause if you don't, I'ma make sure I kill

yo' whole fucking family!" he spat. I laughed and aimed at his head, hitting him twice.

"Aye, June. Nah, man," I heard Dolla say, and Bird grabbed my hand, pulling me away from the little nigga. We jogged back towards the door but the nigga Tez stepped in front of us with two guns aimed at us. I aimed my pistol at his head, and without even thinking, we both let off shots at the same time.

"FUCK!" Bird yelled and stumbled against me. The bullet Tez let off hit Chase in the shoulder, and mine hit Tez in the head. That didn't ease the anger I felt for that nigga, so I let off two more rounds into that nigga's head.

"Fuck, man!" he yelled and I grabbed him by his other arm and helped him up. Looking around, his whole crew was laid out and I sighed.

We walked out of the abandoned warehouse and started to go toward the car. Dropping my arms that were holding Bird up, I slowed down once I saw what Dolla was yelling about.

"Nah, June, get up, bro!" Bird yelled and I turned around. I couldn't even look at my little brother like that. I could tell from the way June was laying against the car that he was gone.

"Help me get 'em up. Man, help me," Bird damn near cried but I couldn't move. My feet were stuck, and the only thing I could hear was Bird screaming for June to get up.

"Aye, we gotta go. Let's go!" Dolla said as the crew came out of hiding and started to pick June's lifeless body up.

"Where the fuck was you niggas at? Huh!" Bird screamed, and I turned around to see Dolla start to lay his crew down one by one until it was just us three standing.

"Let's go," I said and hopped in the back seat next to my little brother. My little brother. FUCK!

CHAPTER 16
Diamond

KNOCK! KNOCK! KNOCK!

"Come in!" I yelled as I wrapped the towel around my body tightly and sat at my vanity. I smiled brightly because I had come far. This time last year, I was locked up and didn't even think I would see life outside the walls. Now, here I was, sitting on over a million dollars of blood money. Money that hundreds of people had lost their lives for. Everything in the world was at the tip of my fingers. I had a sister and brother who adored me and showed me they were riding regardless of anybody. I had friends who were going to war for me, literally! Even though I didn't feel complete yet, my life finally felt like I was seeing the light on the other side of the tunnel. Yeah, shit between Sasha and I wasn't all good, but I saw us getting it right in time.

"Happy birthday, love." Fats' voice brought me out of my daydream, and I pulled the towel around my body tighter. I blushed, thinking about the way our date ended and stood up.

He set the bags down on my bed and pulled me into a hug. I could smell his Burberry cologne and damn near melted in his arms.

"You smell so good." I almost moaned and he laughed and pulled away from me.

"You look beautiful," he complimented and I blushed. My makeup was done perfectly, and my hair was pinned up in tight curls.

"I'm not even dressed yet." I blushed and walked towards the bed so I saw what he had gotten me.

"You didn't have to get all these things," I said and he smiled and grabbed my hands. Fats pushed himself in between my legs and I instantly pulled him closer to me. Fats lifted my head so we could stare into each other's eyes and he brought his lips to mine.

"What... what are you..." Before I could even finish my question, Fats had kissed me. His lips were everything I remembered: soft, plump, and juicy. With my tongue in his mouth, I deepened the kiss by lightly sucking on his tongue. Fats pulled me up and reached for the towel. I hesitated at first and he finally pulled it off, dropping it to the ground. Fats stood back, taking my whole body in and I thanked God I had gone and gotten a fresh wax earlier today. Licking his lips, Fats quickly came out of his shirt. Tattoos covered his chest and stomach, and I envisioned my name on the bare spot on his neck. I climbed into bed and spread my legs wide to give him a perfect view of my bald kitty. Fats smirked and stepped out of his pants and my mouth hung, slightly amazed by how huge he was. What's that saying? Going to see a man about a horse. They had to be talking about Fats because he was indeed hung like a horse.

Fats stood at the edge of my bed, stroking himself as I crawled to him slowly. Replacing his hands with mine, I slowly massaged his dick until it was rock hard. Letting a little spit drip from my mouth onto his tip, he exhaled slowly. Meaty, long, and thick veins, just how I liked it. I smiled and licked from the base to the tip.

"Sssss," Fats hissed, and when I sucked on the tip lightly, I felt his body tense. Taking inch by inch into my mouth, I relaxed my throat as I comfortably stuffed my mouth with his dick.

"Fuck," he growled lowly. I stroked him slowly as I sucked and licked his shaft. Pulling him out of my mouth, I got on my knees and pulled the pin out of my hair so my curls could fall. Fats grabbed a handful of my curls and kissed me sloppily. Slapping his hard-on across my lips, I happily took him all in and he slowly glided me to the speed he liked. Fucking my face, I was happy I knew how to hold my breath and breathe out of my nose.

"Fuck," he moaned as I reached under me and started to slowly rub my clit in a circular motion. The more he fucked my face, the more I fucked myself, and in no time, we both started to cum at the same time. I happily swallowed every drop and Fats smiled lovingly. I laughed a little because I was about to turn his world upside down.

"Turn around," he ordered. "Ass up, face down," he said and I did what I was told, feeling him poke at my entrance.

"Aw, shit," I moaned as he pushed in, giving me all ten inches. Matching thrust for thrust, I threw it back. Fats flipped me over in one quick move and re-entered me missionary style. Kissing all over his tattoos, I wrapped my legs around his waist as he slowly stroked me. Biting down on my shoulder, Fats buried his face in the crack of my neck.

"Oh, God," I mumbled lowly as he hit my spot. Fats was working with a python and he definitely knew how to use it, too. I hadn't had that many sex partners, but I knew the way

Fats was doing my body, nobody had ever done. Slowing down, I knew he didn't want to nut yet, so I started grinding slowly while gripping his dick.

"Shit, Diamond," he damn near cried, and that right there had me cumming all over the bed. Feeling his body jerk on top of me, he let out a loud sigh and fell next to me. I was out of breath, and so was he, but I knew we had a little time to wash off and finish getting ready for the party.

SHOWTIME!

* * *

"I walk around the club fuck everybody.

Can't see, Can't walk, Fuck everybody"

"I'm in my own zone. You got me throwed off," I rapped as I sat next to Fats, who couldn't keep his eyes off me. Every time he looked at me, I just smiled and looked the other way. Looking around the club, I saw everybody from the headquarters was there. It was like the whole city was in attendance. I was a little buzzed, but I made sure I wasn't getting too drunk. Tonight was about one thing and one thing only: revenge!

I wanted revenge so bad, I tasted it. Looking around, it was like our eyes met each other. On cue, my eyes met Alicia's and she smirked before winking. I nodded because this bitch really thought she was untouchable. She walked in with six dudes dressed in black and Sasha came and sat next to me.

"She came here on business. She brought the..." Before Sasha could finish, somebody cleared their throat.

"Sasha, how are you?" a deep voice spoke over the music. I looked up into the darkest set of eyes I'd ever seen. Alicia was right behind him and the men he walked in with.

"Brandon, how are you? This is my daughter, Diamond," Sasha said and I stood up.

"I know who she is," he said and looked me up and down. I laughed because I could tell he wasn't fond of me already. I didn't give a fuck, though. Fuck him and whoever he came with.

"My brothers and I need to speak with you two," Brandon said and waved to the guys he walked in with. Two of the dudes stayed with Alicia and I guessed that was her crew.

"We can go to the office," Sasha said and we followed her out the VIP section, and down a long hallway. I walked first with Sasha and the rest of them behind me. I pushed the door open and found the first seat.

"What do I owe the pleasure of this visit?" Sasha asked, and the one I knew as Brandon stood in front of me.

"You know, your name has been in a lot of shit lately," he told me and I smirked. I crossed one leg over the other.

"Yeah, I bet," I said and he sighed. He looked back at his crew, and in a blink of an eye, his two brothers had grabbed Sasha and had her on her knees. I jumped up before Brandon could even move and had my gun to his head and the other one on the brother who had his gun on Sasha's head.

"All this isn't necessary," I gritted and Brandon's jaw flexed. I could tell he was mad looking down the barrel of the gun. I was going to bust both their heads open if they thought I was going to let him kill my dukes.

"It's really not. We just need an understanding of why you are after Alicia. You know the rules," Brandon asked Sasha and I laughed.

"She does know," I started to say, but Brandon inched closer to me. My gun was pointed exactly in the middle of his forehead.

"I wasn't talking to you, little girl. I was talking to Sash," he spat, then looked at the gun.

"You know what you're doing with that?" he asked and I

smirked. I pushed the gun further into his head and he bit his bottom lip.

"Nigga, I know who you was talking to!" I spat, getting fed up with this shit. "I was talking to you, though. And make one wrong move, this whole office gon' be painted with you and ya mans' blood," I told him. This nigga hunched over laughing. I shook my head and he stepped back.

"What do you have on Alicia?" he asked and crossed his arms in front of him. I must admit, Brandon was sexy as fuck. He was 6'7, at least 275 pounds of pure muscle with chocolate skin, smooth like a Hershey bar without the almonds. He had two Indian braids that went past his shoulder. I saw a small heart tattoo under his eye, and he had a mouth full of gold teeth. This nigga was fine as hell and his brothers who stood behind him were fine, too!

Staring into his eyes, I could tell he could easily take the gun out of my hands and kill me, but he let me have my way for now.

I let the gun fall to my side and sat back down. I sighed and ran my hands down my curls.

"I'm the daughter of Bronco!" I exclaimed.

A puzzled look came across his face as he took what I had just said in.

"Bronco as in my boss Bronco?" he asked as his brothers in the back started whispering to each other.

"Duh, nigga, you don't know yo' boss' kids? And he not yo' boss no more 'cause that BITCH killed him!"

The room got silent and he and his brothers just stared at each other, looking crazy.

He broke the silence when he asked, "So if you really believe that and that's yo' daddy, how are you gonna handle it?"

One of the brothers holding Sasha looked over to Brandon

and said, "She's not gonna handle it because that's not her momma."

Brandon looked at him, then back at me and said, "As far as we know, if Bronco is her daddy, then Alicia is her momma."

Brandon nodded at his brothers, then they let Sasha go, giving me the go-ahead to go get that bitch Alicia.

CHAPTER 17

Chase

"Drive this motherfucker, nigga. He still breathing!" Jersey yelled and hit the back of the seat. Hearing him say that, I turned my whole body around and started to inspect where June had been shot. I saw blood pouring out the back of his neck and Jersey grabbed something from the ground and started to wrap it around his neck.

"Aye, we five minutes away, little bro, stay with me." I felt the tears start to slide down my cheek. I saw on his face he was in pain, but his eyes were closed, and his chest was barely rising and falling.

"Bro, he is dying! Drive this bitch!" Jersey yelled, voice breaking with every word. Pulling out my burner phone, I saw Ginger's name flash across the screen and hang up. She had called over twenty times and my heart dropped in my stomach, feeling like something else was wrong.

"Ma calling... Wh-what do I say?" Jersey said and handed me the phone.

"Ma?" I answered and she screamed.

"Come to the hospital. She took some pills and I was just

in there checking on her. I think... They won't tell me anything," my mama said all in one breath.

"Ma... June got shot. I don't think we're going to make it in time," I finally said. I heard the phone drop and heard her scream.

"Hold on, baby bro. We are almost there," Jersey said. I looked back and saw June's body start to shake as we pulled up to the hospital. Dolla pulled right in front of the emergency doors as I saw my dukes run out with Love and Loyalty in tow.

"WE NEED HELP! AYE, GET ME HELP!" I screamed, looking around for my girl, my wife.

The nurses came rushing out and moved everybody out of the way as they got June out of the car and put him into a bed and rolled him away.

"What happened? What happened to my son?" my mama yelled, grabbing my arm. I couldn't even say. My thoughts were on my little brother.

"Where is Ginger? I asked, looking around. My momma sighed, then faced Jersey. She turned back to me with the saddest, broken eyes I'd ever seen and it hit me—they were there because she had taken some pills.

"Son," I heard my momma say, but I tuned her out, then everything went black.

CHAPTER 18

ASARI

(3 YEARS LATER)

"You look good, Asari, and I've watched you grow tremendously," my therapist said and I smiled. It's been a long, long three years for me. I wasn't the same broken girl at all.

"Today is your death anniversary, and I just wanna see where your head's at," Jen asked and I sighed. A happy sigh. I was happy, happier than I'd been in a very, very long time. I was healthy, I was stronger, and I was engaged. Yes, Jersey decided to propose last year, and of course, I said yes! Most importantly, my family was together and we were good.

"I'm happy, Jennifer. So happy. Like, Jersey loves me and he loves the twins. Like, adores the twins. He loves them more than me." I laughed and she laughed, too.

"I mean, he's supposed to," she said and I smiled.

"I know, but him accepting them made me love him even more. My family is happy. Love and Loyalty graduate in two weeks and they are doing so much better. Even with the shooting and June... You know, everything was rough at first, very rough, but we are good. Chase and Jersey are even back like they never left. You know 'cause they were pretty bad off once Chase told Jersey it was my and his fault that Gin did what she did." I smiled and silently thanked God for bringing my family back together.

"I'm just happy. I didn't ever think I would feel like this. Being so depressed and miserable for so long, Jen, I'm just happy I'm not in that space anymore," I said and she nodded, smiling at me.

"Well, that's all I needed to see and hear. I think your case is closed and I am closing this session," Jen said and I smiled. I stood up and we shook hands before hugging.

"Happy looks good on you," Jen complimented and I smiled and did a spin for her. Gaining my weight back, I was a brick house, for real. My slim-thick frame was extra thick now and I loved the extra weight on me. My once long hair was short, in a pixie cut that shaped my round face. The braces that were once there were now gone and perfectly white teeth were in. I was happy, looking good, and feeling good.

"Thank you. Thank you so much, Jen. I'll see you," I said and grabbed my MCM tote, and walked out. The guards that Jersey had watching me hopped up once I left the office and followed me outside. Brick opened the back door and I slid in and got comfortable for the long ride to the house I shared with my family.

A few months after the kidnapping, Jersey moved us into my own six-bedroom house. I said my own because he made sure it was in my name. I leaned back and pulled my phone out to send Love a text to tell her to take something out for me to cook. Checking my emails, I sighed and stared at the email I had been waiting to receive for the last week.

"This is all my fault." I sighed and rubbed my hands through my hair. I quickly wiped the tears that wanted to fall but they just wouldn't. I wasn't crying anymore. That was all I'd done my entire life. My tears had dried up three years ago when I was tied up in that basement. Shit, my sad tears anyway. If you saw me cry now, they were happy tears.

The night Jersey killed Tez was a night I would never ever forget. I couldn't even imagine the state Mama Laura was in to have to make that call and instead get the call that June had been shot. The usual forty-five-minute drive turned into twenty-four minutes and I smiled looking at my whole family in the yard as we pulled up and parked.

Mama Laura walked towards the tables the guys were sitting at with Love and Loyalty on her side. My smile brightened when I saw Jersey reach out and grab hold of our three-year-old daughter Brooklyn and sat her in June's lap as he wheeled him to the table. Our three-year-old son Harlem chased Autumn around as she pushed him down in the grass. I saw him pick up something and throw it at her as she laughed and ran around her daddy and uncles.

"Slow down, Harlem!" Mama L ordered and my son immediately stopped running and went to go sit with Jersey and his uncles.

Let's just say we thought shit was going to go back to normal when Tez died, but shit was still bad. Just imagine someone coming into your life, killing your parents, your siblings, and your aunty, then turning your best friend against you, and that wasn't even the half. Tez shot Jersey and June and almost killed him, burnt our house down, then kidnapped, raped, and tortured me. Even after this nigga had done all of that to me and my family, he still haunted me from hell. Four months after the kidnapping, I found out I was fifteen weeks pregnant with twins, a boy and a girl.

Twins? How the fuck was I going to tell my nigga who had gone through hell and back with me in so little time that I was pregnant by the nigga who had caused us hell. I just knew he was going to leave me, but nah, Jersey was with whatever I was with. I wanted to keep the babies? He was signing birth certificates. I wanted to abort mission? He was taking me to Chicago for the abortion. Four months later, I welcomed a healthy baby girl who goes by the name Brooklyn and a healthy badass little boy who goes by the name Harlem into this world. My son and daughter came out looking exactly like me. Dark skin, curly hair, deep dimples, my color eyes and all. We were triplets, for real. Thank God, because I didn't know how I was going to feel looking at replicas of the man who had taken everything in this world from me. God had other plans, though. I knew having them was my rainbow after the storm. Jersey loved those two babies with all his heart, too.

If I didn't know by then that we were meant to be, at that moment, I knew Jersey and I were soulmates.

"Mommy!" Brooklyn screamed and I smiled and waved. Jersey blew me a kiss and jogged to greet me as I stepped out of the car.

"How was your session?" he asked and I smiled and felt butterflies in my stomach. The same feeling I got every time Jersey was near. This time, the feeling was for something different.

"What is all this?" I asked, talking about the little picnic set up and our small little family.

"You know what today is. It's a celebration of life, for you," he said and kissed my lips. I pulled him into a hug and he held me tight.

"Girl, come on, we're ready to eat!" Ginger yelled and I laughed at her big ass. Ginger was nine months pregnant and was about to bust and Chase couldn't wait to finally meet his first little one.

"Wassup, sis?" he greeted and pulled me into a hug. I must admit, I wasn't his favorite person at all. Especially after the day June got shot. Ginger snuck out and got an abortion. Her excuse was she didn't think they were ready for kids with everything that had been going on. Chase blamed me and Jersey because shit, Tez was after me so that brought problems to everyone around me. He and Gin did break up, but they didn't divorce. He was hurt about the abortion but they worked shit out and now she was welcoming B.C. at any moment.

"Hey, baby bro." I kissed June's head and then kissed my baby girl Brooklyn's head.

June survived his shooting, but it left him paralyzed from the waist down. It didn't break him, though. He was still the same hot head with a big pistol, as he would say. He just wasn't in the streets anymore for the sake of Autumn. I could say he was happier than he ever was, too, despite being in a wheelchair.

"How are you feeling?" Mama Laura asked and I smiled and hugged her tightly.

"Actually, I have some news," I said and the table grew quiet. I sighed and smiled. I had the nerve to want to end my life and leave these wonderful people. My people.

When Jersey left to go handle Tez, I decided that I didn't want to live anymore. I found some pills in Laura's bathroom and took as much as I could. I was ready to end it all. I knew Love and Loyalty would've been better off without me. I knew Jersey deserved a woman who didn't bring so much chaos and trouble into his life. I knew I was hurting and didn't want to endure that pain anymore. God said sike and kept me here. He kept me here because He knew I was bringing two beautiful lives into this world soon. He knew Love and Loyalty couldn't take any more death. He also knew that Jersey and I were meant to be together forever. He couldn't hurt him like that by taking me. I was just happy He saw fit to keep me here through all the bullshit I'd been through.

"I just got news that... that I'm pregnant," I said and Jersey laughed and jumped up. He hugged me so tight, spinning me around and I laughed. When I had the twins, I had hella complications and the doctors basically told me I would never be able to get pregnant again. Well, I guess God wanted to expand the family because here I was with child number three. I was more than happy.

"Damn, we're late again," I heard Dolla say, slamming the car door. He helped his girlfriend Macy out of the car and she put her hand on her small basketball of a stomach and waved at everyone. Macy was my nurse at the hospital and we became good friends. I kind of played matchmaker and hooked Macy and Dolla up and they'd been rocking ever since. I knew he needed a distraction from the shit with his pops. Then finding out his mother had been killed a little after his dad, he needed someone. Macy came in and saved him and they had been on each other's side ever since. Pretty soon, Dolla was welcoming his first kid, a girl, into the world.

"Yes, y'all are. Hey, Macy, Asari just announced that she is with child," Mama Laura said and clapped again.

"Damn, y'all ain't done yet? Congrats, sis," Dolla said and pulled me into a hug after I hugged Macy. I playfully rolled my eyes at his comment and smiled as Macy rubbed my small stomach.

"Girl, I hope you are ready. I'm only three months in and look like I'm six," Macy said and I laughed.

"Girl, I was that big at three months with the twins. Trust me, I can handle anything," I said and Jersey smiled and pulled me into him.

"Hopefully, it is twins," he whispered and I damn near choked on my spit.

"Aw, nah. You see how bad that little boy is? Where is he at anyways?" I asked. As soon as I looked around, I saw Harlem come from out of nowhere with the water hose, spraying everybody and everything.

"HARLEM!" Jersey yelled and I shook my head and followed the ladies as they ran towards the house. My life was definitely a book. I was just waiting for Miss Tina B to turn it into a movie.

CHAPTER 19
Nova

Walking into the club, it was packed as fuck. This was my last night in Indianapolis and I was happy because my girl was finally getting closure tonight and I was starting over with my sons. I had also finally told my people and friends about Nassir and Nas. My sons were my whole world. Ever since the day I asked Ashley to think about moving away with me, I had been to see my sons every single day. They even came and stayed the weekend with me. I knew the life I lived here, I wasn't fit to be a mother 24/7 so Ashley still had them most of the time. Now that I was finally done with these streets and was moving far the fuck away, I was so happy Ashley agreed to move with me.

All I needed was Diamond to bring her ass, too. I hadn't told her about the move yet because I wanted to see where her head was. My pops was the only one who knew I was leaving.

He didn't take it well, only because he knew the damage I was doing by leaving. Queenz was a one-way out thing, and if Sasha knew I was leaving, she wouldn't hesitate to have my body cut in pieces and sent to my pops. I was willing to take that chance, plus, I knew if Diamond came with me, Sasha would just let us go. Shit, at least I hoped so. This time tomorrow, I would be in the house I purchased in Hawaii with my sons and their granny. I couldn't wait.

Stepping into the VIP section, I stopped mid-step when I saw Alicia standing there like she owned the section.

Treasure came to me and hooked her arm with mine.

"This scary ass bitch brought Brandon nem with her. He is in the back, talking to my dukes and Diamond now," Treasure said and I nodded.

"I don't give a fuck who she brought. That bitch ain't leaving out of here alive!" I spat, ready to put a bullet in her head for my girl. I didn't give a fuck about no rules or who she was! That bitch had my friend fucked up and I would worry about the consequences later.

"Nah, just stay cool. We stick to the plan. Just know I got that bitch ass nigga standing next to her," Treasure said and I smiled.

"And I got the other one," I said and we shook up. I went to join the crew in the section, and we started chilling. The atmosphere was so motherfucking thick. Everybody sat with their hands on their pistols, ready for whatever.

My mind was on overload and all I could think about was my sons and sitting on the beach somewhere relaxing. I pulled my phone out to check the time and saw that I had several missed calls from Ashley. Standing up, I walked to the back with my phone up to one ear and my finger to the other to muffle the club sounds. Stepping near a door, my son Nas came over the speaker. I opened the closed door and stepped into the small closet for privacy.

"Hey, mommy. We were just calling because we wanted to say goodnight. We love you and can't wait to see you for breakfast," his sweet little voice said, and I smiled.

"Goodnight, son, I love y'all so much and I will see you soon," I said and we hung up. I held the phone to my heart and smiled. My sons were so sweet and innocent. They loved me no matter how much time passed, and I was grateful for them. Turning around, I was met with the barrel of a gun at the middle of my forehead.

I sighed heavily because I had just got caught slipping bad as fuck. I tried to reach for my gun on the side of me, but in one swift motion, a burning sensation hit my throat, which made me drop.

"I know you ain't think you could quit us and there would be no consequences. See you in hell," I heard before the last person I thought I would see threw the knife next to me. He turned to walk away, but not before he raised the gun and shot, leaving me with my final thought... Damn.

CHAPTER 20
Diamond

Walking back to the club, I saw Alicia looking at me, smirking. She thought she was untouchable, but the whole time, her whole life was about to be snatched from her. I saw everybody in place and held my hands up for them to stand down. Plans had changed. Walking up to Alicia, my stepbrother, and another nigga, I stood right in front of them.

"I should do you like I did Lance, but I don't wanna do you like that," I said to Landan and his eyes softened at the mention of his bitch ass brother. I smirked and gave the signal. Before he could even respond, Jewel had dropped him with one quick shot, then did the same to the other nigga.

Alicia looked around and was about to reach for her gun, but I held mine up to her head first and stepped forward.

"You know who I am? You're not gonna pull that trigger." She smirked and I laughed. I laughed to keep from crying because this bitch had raised me as her own, and took care of me, whole time she hated me because of my pops. She wanted everything my pops left me. She tried to kill me while I was locked up and made my life a living hell. This was my mother, the only mother I knew! How could God make somebody so wicked!

"Nah, do you know who I am?" I asked and smirked. "I know you didn't think you would get away with killing my fucking daddy, mother?" I asked and her face dropped. She looked around and saw everybody from Queenz and the head niggas in charge were standing around us. No music was playing, and out of my peripheral, I saw the club being cleared out.

Realizing that she was all alone, she looked down at her son and charged me, knocking the gun out of my hands and me to the ground.

Alicia got on top of me and started to hit me with all her might. I quickly wrapped one leg around her and pulled her on the side of me and kicked her in the stomach. We both stood up at the same time and she reached for her pistol on her side. It must've fallen off during the scuffle because she put her hands up in a fighting stance.

Doing the same, we started walking in circles and I easily threw the first two hits, connecting to her face. Drawing blood from her nose turnt me up, so I went in and threw another two punches, only connecting the first one. She threw a jab, dazing me a little bit. This old ass bitch had some strength on her.

She reached to her other side, pulled out a knife, and smirked. I nodded and put my hands back up. She rushed me, swinging the knife from side to side and I jumped back with every swing. With all my strength, I hit her once and she fell on her ass. She hopped back up quickly, and before she could swing the knife again, I hit her and she fell again. This time, I kicked the knife from her hands and got on top of her. I used the move that Treasure had taught me and put my knees on her arms so she couldn't use her arms. She smiled with blood in her mouth and just laid there.

"You don't got the fucking guts to kill me." She spat in my

face. I quickly wiped the blood and spit from my face and reached for the knife she had.

"Nah, I didn't have the guts but you turned me into somebody I never thought I'd be," I told her truthfully as I grabbed her by the hair and took the knife across her neck. Alicia's eyes popped open and I saw the blood gush from her neck. It didn't stop me, though. I stuck the knife as far as I could into her heart and stood up.

"Welcome to the top," Brandon said and held his hand out for me to shake. I ignored his hand and walked out of the club. I was finally at peace now.

Epilogue

ONE YEAR LATER...

"I wanna thank everyone that's here today. If you are here, then I find you worthy to continue to be a part of my organization. There are a lot of new faces, a lot of new rules, and it's a whole new operation. My story is built on blood, sweat, and loyalty! The ones here are who I saw fit to be a part of my story. To show my appreciation, I have some ladies bringing gift bags around the room," I told my crew.

Last year, I walked out of the club a whole new person. I wasn't the same Diamond at all. Now, I was the fucking head bitch in charge. The HBIC of a multi-million-dollar company. Some shit I didn't fucking know about. When Brandon told me I had no choice but to take my seat as the head, I jumped in the fucking game headfirst, no safety net. Nobody was here to hold my hand and tell me what I needed to do so I fumbled the bag for months, lost a lot of distributors, and even lost some people who I thought I would have on my side forever. Speaking of that...

"OG Ciro," I spoke and waved him closer to me. I stood up in front of the chair I was sitting in and walked closer to him. I saw my momma Sasha shaking her head but I smirked and sighed. I know she didn't think I was letting this slide. Out of all things, she knew I couldn't let this one thing slide.

"Yes, boss lady," he spoke in broken English. I made sure his family was attending this meeting for this special reason.

"I've been beating the streets heavily for the last year, trying to find your daughter," I said and waved for his wife to come to the front.

"I'm still trying to figure out how you said she was leaving with her sons and leaving the game," I said and he looked around nervously.

"I promised my momma I wouldn't touch a hair on your head because of the love she had for you but I don't think you should be living anymore for taking Nova," I said and the whispers started.

"Quiet, please," I said calmly and the whole building hushed. Tears filled my eyes and I let them fall freely. I put my hand on my back because my body was tired. My heart was broken when I finally got the cameras restored from the night of my birthday. It took a whole fucking year for me to find someone to hack into some shit and get deleted footage on where Nova went. Imagine my surprise when my girl walked off to talk on the phone and her pops came from no-fucking-where and followed her. She was never seen after that.

"So with that being said, I'm giving anyone from Headshot Queenz or the Leornada family my blessing to avenge Nova's death. He can walk out of here freely, still do business with us, and be a free man. It's y'all call," I said, looking at my people.

"Before anyone from Queenz stands up, just know Sasha isn't clearing it so you will be going against her wishes," I said and Marisol, who I now knew as Nova's little cousin stood tall and stood by Nova's mother. Jessica from Queenz walked and stood on the other side of Nova's mother.

"Jess, there ain't no coming back," I said and she nodded. Nova's father dropped to his knees. Jess was the first to pull her knife and stab him in the stomach. He grunted but never folded. The next was Marisol, who pulled her knife and stabbed him in the back. Nova's mother got on her knees in front of OG Ciro and leaned in close. I thought she was about to kiss him but she didn't. She spat in his face and gave him one stab to the heart that brought him crashing down to his side. Each of them took turns stabbing him until his soul left his body.

A crew came and grabbed the body and I slowly walked back to my seat and sat down. Fats rubbed my back and kissed my cheek.

"Hurry up so we can get back home," he whispered and I nodded.

"As you all see, I gave you a gift. As of now, I am on a leave of absence to enjoy the rest of my pregnancy and to welcome a healthy baby boy into this world." I smiled and Fats rubbed my stomach. "Everyone in this room knows how to get in touch with me. I will see everyone in exactly six weeks. This meeting is over," I said and everyone started to disappear. My momma was the first to approach me.

It was still weird as hell to know that Sasha was my real mother but I was happy that she walked into that visitation room. I was even happier that she fought for me. Fought so that I could be free. I loved Sasha. It took us a long time to get where we were now but I was glad shit was how it was! She had even stepped down from Headshot Queenz and helped me run shit.

Treasure and Jewel were literally my best friends. Jewel was thirty-eight hot when Fats and I made it official and even madder when I found out I was pregnant. Getting pregnant so soon wasn't part of the plan, especially with us being so new and not married but Fats showed me every day that I was the one for him and he loved me dearly. I must say, my life was complete and I was happier than I'd ever been in life. I was just happy I could finally put this pen and pad down and focus on myself, my man, and our baby boy.

THE END!

Want to be a part of Grand Penz Publications?

To submit your manuscript to Grand Penz Publications, please send the first three chapters and synopsis to grandpenzpublications@gmail.com

www.ingramcontent.com/pod-product-compliance
Lightning Source LLC
LaVergne TN
LVHW010107170826
845678LV00012B/2280

* 9 7 9 8 8 4 9 4 8 3 1 1 5 *